## "Tell me what's going on," Tate demanded.

Stephanie didn't look at him. "Bittman wants something from me." She turned her face to his, and he saw for the first time the gleam of tears there. "He drove my brother off the road and took Dad."

"I'm sorry." For one crazy moment, he wanted to wrap her up in an embrace. "How does it fit together? What is Bittman after?"

"I can't tell you any more."

He folded his arms. "I want to know what's going on, and you're going to tell me."

Her eyes glittered. "I wasn't supposed to get anyone involved, or he'll kill my father."

"Too late. I'm involved."

Her eyes grew cold. "No you're not, Tate," she said as she pushed by him, leaving a tantalizing whiff of the cinnamon fragrance she always wore.

Why, he wondered, could he pass through his day without remembering so much as what he had for lunch—but he could recall every detail of Stephanie's face after seeing her for only a few moments in the past four years?

## Books by Dana Mentink

Love Inspired Suspense

*Killer Cargo*
*Flashover*
*Race to Rescue*
*Endless Night*
*Betrayal in the Badlands*
*Turbulence*
*Buried Truth*
*Escape from the Badlands*
\*Lost Legacy
\*Dangerous Melody

\*Treasure Seekers

### DANA MENTINK

lives in California, where the weather is golden and the cheese is divine. Her family includes two girls (affectionately nicknamed Yogi and Boo Boo). Papa Bear works for the fire department; he met Dana doing a dinner theater production of *The Velveteen Rabbit*. Ironically, their parts were husband and wife.

Dana is a 2009 American Christian Fiction Writers Book of the Year finalist for romantic suspense and an award winner in the Pacific Northwest Writers Literary Contest. Her novel *Betrayal in the Badlands* won a 2010 *RT Book Reviews* Reviewers' Choice Award. She has enjoyed writing a mystery series for Barbour Books and more than ten novels to date for Harlequin's Love Inspired Suspense line.

She spent her college years competing in speech and debate tournaments all around the country. Besides writing, she busies herself teaching elementary school and reviewing books for her blog. Mostly, she loves to be home with her family, including a dog with social anxiety problems, a chubby box turtle and a quirky parakeet.

Dana loves to hear from her readers via her website at www.danamentink.com.

# DANGEROUS MELODY

## DANA MENTINK

Love Inspired

Recycling programs
for this product may
not exist in your area.

™ LOVE INSPIRED BOOKS

ISBN-13: 978-0-373-44513-4

DANGEROUS MELODY

www.LoveInspiredBooks.com

Printed in U.S.A.

Brothers and sisters, I do not consider myself yet to have taken hold of it. But one thing I do: Forgetting what is behind and straining toward what is ahead, I press on toward the goal to win the prize for which God has called me heavenward in Christ Jesus.

—*Philippians* 3:13–14

To my dear friend Patsy in Waxahachie.
You are an encouragement and a blessing to me.

# ONE

The piercing ring of the phone made Stephanie Gage almost drop the box she was carrying. Her mind jumped to a horrible conclusion. Bittman had found her. Again. Now it would start all over, the phone calls, the flowers left on her doorstep, the feeling that she was being watched. Stephanie felt a flush of anger and shame. Her decision to work for Joshua Bittman had been disastrous. For her it was a job, for Bittman, the beginning of an obsession—and he'd stalked her steadily since she'd quit his employ two years before.

She tried to rein in the rampaging fear, to remember the courageous woman she used to be. How had he found her so quickly? Her new number was unlisted, her small Victorian, a quiet retreat from the hustle and bustle of the Mission district, quiet and anonymous—or so she'd thought.

She was about to snatch up the phone and let the fury fuel her words when she recognized her older brother Victor's number on the caller ID. Chagrined at her own paranoia, she answered.

"I'm in the car," Victor said. "Took the scenic route along Highway 1. The view is spectacular and no traffic. Guess what, sis?"

Stephanie heard only joy in his voice. It reverberated through her like the cool breeze of the San Francisco morning.

"Brooke and I set a date for the wedding," Victor told her. "And our hard-to-please dad has given his stamp of approval, now that he's finally met her."

"Not that it matters," her father chimed in. "No one listens to me anyway."

She laughed, pushing back her messy black hair. "I'm listening, finally." Though she could force a brave tone, the mental scars would never fade, even if the memories did, if and when the fear finally abated.

"I don't think you've given up your rebellious side yet, little lady," her father added.

*Little lady.* She'd just celebrated her twenty-sixth birthday.

"Did you call Luca?" Her other brother had been close to marrying a few times, but now he was immersed in their activities at Treasure Seekers, the private agency run by the three Gage siblings dedicated to finding treasures for select clients. Luca would be just as pleased that Victor was tying the knot with Brooke, a woman they'd met during their last treasure hunt, whose father Victor had wrongly believed was a criminal.

"I'll call him next. He's probably busy trying to find our next case," Victor said.

"Hard to top securing a twenty-million-dollar painting."

Victor chuckled. "He was blabbering about an emerald collection when I left for southern California."

She marveled at his voice, so light and joyful. Somehow knowing Victor's heart was mended made her own broken relationship easier to endure. Pushing the image of Tate out of her mind, she forced a happier tone. "I'm thrilled for you." She spoke louder, over the background noise, which seemed to have edged up a notch on his end.

He started to laugh but broke off suddenly. "Hang on. What is…?" The noise swelled into a screech of tires.

Fingers suddenly icy, Stephanie clutched the phone. "Victor?"

Her heart fractured, along with the sound of shattering glass. "Victor!" she screamed. "Dad. What's happening?"

A hideous scraping tore at her ears. She yelled something into the phone, incoherent syllables, fear and helplessness making her words shrill. Tinkling glass, the protest of distressed metal, a massive thunk and the sound of tires sliding over gravel. She thought she heard her father cry out, and she squeezed the phone in a death grip.

"Answer me," she screamed, heart thundering against her ribs.

Then the noises faded into a soft crunch of gravel. Quieter, softer until there was no sound at all. No sound, except the violent hammering of her own heart. Her mouth would not form the words for a long moment. "Victor? Dad? Are you all right?"

Metal creaked, the sound of a door opening. Hope rose inside her. "Tell me you're all right," she whispered.

A voice came on the line. Cold, musical and chillingly familiar. "Stephanie, I have your father. There's something I need you to do for me. I will call you back in exactly four hours," Bittman said. "Mention me to anyone, and Wyatt Gage will die." The phone clicked off.

Her frantic call to the police revealed that a passing motorist had reported the wreck and a Lifeflight helicopter was transporting Victor to the nearest trauma center. Another call to her father's cell phone went unanswered. With numb fingers, she dialed Luca.

Joshua Bittman could not have her father.

Because if he did…

"Hey, sis. What's up?"

She pictured him, a bigger, blonder version of their dark-haired older brother, his green eyes sparkling with mischief.

*What's up?*

She knew Luca. She knew without question that if she told him the truth, he would summon the police and personally storm Bittman's Hillsborough mansion. But she also knew Joshua Bittman. He would not hesitate to kill Wyatt Gage and Luca in a heartbeat to get whatever it was that he wanted. "Victor was on the phone with me and he crashed," she said, stomach twisting. She gave him the details, leaving out any mention of their father being in the car.

Luca exhaled, voice tight with emotion. "Did you call Dad?"

*There's no use,* she wanted to shout. *Bittman has Dad.* The words stuck in her throat, but she finally choked out a reply. "No answer."

"My buddy's on duty today, he's a Lifeflight nurse. I'll call him on my way to the hospital and call you back."

He hung up, and she began to pace in frantic circles. The minutes slowed to a crawl as she tried to decide what to do that wouldn't make the situation worse. After what seemed like an eternity, Luca called again.

"My buddy said they admitted Victor and took him in for emergency surgery. He's…been badly hurt."

The words lanced through her. Brooke and Victor were supposed to be starting a new life together, and Brooke deserved it as much as Victor, having seen her ailing father narrowly escape false imprisonment for a robbery. The Treasure Seekers Agency had recovered all manner of rich prizes, but their last adventure to locate Brooke's father's missing painting was far more treacherous than any they'd undertaken. Floods, tunnel collapses and a murder seemed like distant memories now.

Victor was the backbone of the agency. She flashed on a memory of him and their father, knee-deep in piles of old books, hunting out references to a priceless stamp. Terror about Victor's prognosis and her father's whereabouts made her hands ice cold, her breath short.

She realized Luca was talking.

She jerked. "What?"

"I said I'll call Brooke and meet you at the hospital." He paused. "Keep it together, Steph. You're strong. Remember that."

"We both know that's not true." She'd collapsed when Tate Fuego had walked out of her life, descending lower and lower until she found herself fully entwined in Joshua Bittman's nightmare world.

"Steph? Are you there?"

She heard the edge of a deeper concern written in Luca's voice, underneath the calm exterior.

Could it be that her father had been injured but made it out of the car? Was he wandering around the crash area in need of help? Her heart leaped. Maybe Bittman was bluffing. Maybe he hadn't snatched him after all, and she was wrong.

The hope lasted less than a minute before it dried up and disappeared. The truth left a sour taste in her mouth.

Bittman did many things, but one thing he did not do was bluff.

He also did not threaten.

He punished. He was a billionaire many times over, and she'd suspected he'd paid officials to look the other way on his business dealings. Worse, she'd known people who'd crossed Bittman to simply disappear with no evidence on dirty Bittman's well-manicured hands—vanished as if they'd never existed.

She checked her watch. Three-and-a-half hours to go. As the little hand ticked away the seconds, something shifted inside Stephanie. The fear coursing through her body coalesced into another emotion, white-hot and razor sharp. She would not sit by while Bittman turned her life upside down again.

She was done running, done hiding. He would pay for what he had done to Victor. He would deliver her father unharmed.

"I have to go somewhere," she said.

"Come again?"

She braced herself. "Go to the hospital. I'll call you when I can."

"Steph," he said. "You're in trouble. I can hear it in your voice. Whatever it is, let me help you."

*Not this time, big brother.*

A few minutes after two o'clock, Tate Fuego pulled his motorcycle to a stop in the shelter of massive trees lining the gate that circled Joshua Bittman's mansion. The building itself was a domed-top monstrosity of white stone, flanked by stretches of impeccably manicured lawns and a rectangular pond that reflected the building. A long driveway was empty except for a mint condition Mustang GT 350 and a black Mercedes.

Tate saw no sign of his sister Maria's car, though he knew she'd been a regular at Bittman's place. Her phone call three days prior scared him. Her normally upbeat personality was gone, and the woman on the line sounded irrational and unsteady, though she would not tell him why. Then nothing. No response to his texts, and no one answering the door at her apartment. He ground his teeth. She shouldn't have gotten involved with Bittman in the first place, and if he ever got a chance, he'd take Stephanie to task for introducing them.

The breeze teased ripples into the water of the pond, mirroring the discomfort in his own gut at the thought of Stephanie. Her dark eyes flashed in his memory, and he blinked away the pain. At the sound of an approaching engine, he rolled his bike farther back into the shadows. A van rumbled slowly by with *American Pool Company* printed on the exterior. When it pulled to a stop at the intercom, the driver, a stocky, crew-cut man with a face corrugated by wrinkles, leaned out to speak into the box.

"Pool service," he heard the driver bark, with a Spanish accent.

Tate grabbed the handle to the rear doors of the van and eased it down, wondering if he would be caught. In a moment he was safely inside. The guy parked the van and headed for the pool with a water test kit. Tate slipped out the back and ran for the nearest side entrance. In a place this ritzy, he knew interior security cameras would pick him up quickly, but he didn't need much time. One minute with Bittman, he thought grimly, was all he'd need.

He found himself in a gleaming kitchen, which was thankfully empty. The place was quiet, eerily so. Not one housekeeper in sight? No butlers or maids? Strangest of all, no burly security personnel barreling toward him.

His instincts prickled.

Muscles taut, he crept up the stairs and heard a murmur of voices. Heading swiftly along the hall, he came to a large window that looked down on an atrium. Trees that had to be at least twenty feet thrust upward toward the enormous skylights that bathed the space in pale sun. He was startled when a blue blur whizzed by his face. A parrot with feathers the color of the sky and intense yellow eyes peered at him from a branch. Below, through the screen of foliage, something else moved, this time of the two-legged variety.

Tate retraced his steps downstairs, skirting the lower floor hallway until he found the entrance to the atrium. The glass door was closed but not locked. Opening it as quietly as he could, Tate entered the warm, humid enclosure.

The parrot noises were varied and loud. Shrieks, raucous squawks and even some words rang through the space. An Elvis song, Maria's favorite.

Teeth gritted, he ducked between the spiked leaves and

headed deeper into the bizarre tropical room. Branches crackled on his left, and he froze. Bird or Bittman, he could not tell. He passed a long metal pole with a mirror affixed to the end, leaning against the wall. Some sort of device so Bittman could check on his nesting birds? He turned to head back to the door when he felt a cold circle of metal pressed to his neck.

"Turn around," a voice growled.

A burly man, a head shorter than Tate, held a gun level with Tate's chest. He spoke into a radio. "I've got a guy in the aviary, and the girl is breaking down the door on the second floor."

*Breaking down the door.*

His brain filled in the rest. His sister. Kept here. That explained why she didn't return his calls, why she was no longer using her cell. The man was pointing him toward the door, and Tate could see the muscled arms under the suit coat.

He stepped back and raised a hand. "I don't want trouble. I'll go."

*After I find my sister.*

He moved toward the door, Suit Guy a couple of paces behind him. Tate edged closer to the glass wall until he was alongside the pole he'd seen earlier.

"Get going," the man grumbled.

Tate did, as he grabbed the pole and swung it in a wide circle, knocking the man to his knees. When he completed the turn, Tate raced to the door. Pole still in his hands, he cleared the doors and pushed them closed, wedging the pole through the double handles. He made for the stairs at a dead run, ignoring the pain shooting up his leg.

The pole wasn't strong, and the guy was burly. He'd be through in a few good pushes.

Clearing the stairs, Tate charged toward the sound of splintering wood.

\* \* \*

Stephanie raised the upholstered chair again, part of her brain noting that the legs of the nineteenth century Danish piece were starting to come apart. She quickly scanned the richly appointed sitting room. She knew Bittman must be watching via the extensive network of security cameras. He was playing some kind of sick game, allowing her to walk in past all the security she knew he had in place. The mansion itself made her nauseous, recalling how she had played into Bittman's schemes, been tricked by his combination of massive intellect and complete indifference to anyone but himself. And her.

Shutting her mind to the memories, she turned again to the locked door at the far side of the room and pushed to see if she had weakened it. After a thorough search of all the other rooms on the floor, this was the last. It also housed the only door she'd found locked, which meant there was something in it she wasn't meant to see. It was now almost four hours after the accident, and the mansion was the likeliest place to have taken his prisoner. Only a quarter of an hour remained until Bittman's promised contact.

Putting down the chair for a moment, she slammed a palm against the wood door.

"Daddy?" she called. Ears straining, she heard nothing. He could be gagged. Or worse.

She grabbed hold of the chair and raised it aloft, knowing it could be a matter of moments before Bittman or his lackeys stopped her.

Before she could smash it again into the locked master bedroom door, someone caught her arm. She shifted, turning to use the chair to strike at her opponent, but whoever it was ducked and the blow sailed over his head. Suddenly, she was pinned face-first against the wall by a strong set of arms, her cheek pressed against the wood. She struggled to free an elbow to bring it into her attacker's ribs when, just as abruptly, she was released. Knocked off balance, she readied a front-arm strike and whirled around, finding herself looking into the shocked face of Tate Fuego.

His hands dropped to his sides and he moved slightly back, as if he would turn away, but he didn't. Those eyes kept burning into her, taking in the scar on her cheekbone, churning her feelings into a tidal wave that threatened to overwhelm her. She kicked the ruined chair aside.

"What are you doing here?" Her voice sounded tremulous in her own ears, which infuriated her.

Tate didn't answer, instead turning around and shutting the double doors behind him, locking them and pulling a chair over to wedge against the wood. "Going to have company in a few minutes."

"What are you doing?" she demanded again.

He rounded on her. "Looking for Maria."

"I haven't seen her," Stephanie said.

Tate's broad shoulders tensed. "Why are you breaking down the door?"

"Because…" What should she tell him? She was searching Bittman's house? And what would be a reasonable explanation for that? She had to get Tate to leave. Bittman was clear that no one should know about her father, or there would be deadly consequences. "You've got to go, Tate."

He folded his arms. "Not until you've explained why you're bent on smashing down this door."

She sucked in a deep breath. "It's not your concern."

"There's a guy coming up the stairs in about another minute to throw me off the property. Bittman knows about my sister, and now I see you're involved with him somehow, so I'm making it my concern."

Stephanie's stomach tightened, and a sense of urgency

nearly choked her. She moved to him, putting a hand on his solid chest. "Tate, please. You need to leave."

He gave her that slow smile, a shadow of the crooked, cocky grin from the time before everything had fallen apart between them. His hand touched hers gently. Then he moved off, sat in a high-backed leather chair and put up his booted feet on the pristine table. "I don't think so, Steph." He stretched his arms behind his neck, giving her that grin. "Fuego Demolitions is between contracts right now. I've got all the time in the world."

The outer door began to shudder as someone yanked the knob.

# TWO

Stephanie felt a scream building as she ran to him and grabbed his wrist. His hands closed around hers, callused and strong. She knew it was going to be impossible to move him, but panic overrode her common sense. "Tate…"

A fist pounded on the door.

"Open up," shouted an unfamiliar voice.

She looked wildly at Tate.

He shrugged. "Bittman's security guy. I guess he made it out of the birdcage."

She had only moments. Tate or no Tate, she had to get to her father. Stephanie ran to the scarred door and screamed through it again. "Daddy," she yelled. "Answer me."

The words electrified Tate. He was on his feet and next to her in a second. "Your father's in there?"

"I'm not sure, but I've got to know."

He grabbed her arm. "Steph, what's going on?'

"Get out of my way." She shook him off and picked up the chair again.

He stopped her hand for the second time, pulling a pocketknife from his jeans. "Faster," he said, applying the blade to the hinge.

The pounding on the door was loud now, then it stopped

abruptly. A crash of wood on wood made Stephanie jump. "He'll be through in a minute."

"Me, too," Tate said, popping loose the pin.

Stephanie saw the outer doors to the suite beginning to weaken under the assault of a foot or shoulder. With a crack, a booted foot came through a ragged gap.

Tate lifted the door free, and Stephanie tumbled in with Tate right behind her. There was a king-size master bed in disarray, sheets and blankets twisted. She ran into the adjoining bathroom, where she found a small basin and some bandages. Heart thundering, she returned to the bedroom to find Tate examining something.

He held up a pair of plastic restraints.

Her heart plummeted. The crack of wood in the outer room meant the security guy was nearly through.

She ran to the bed and felt the covers. "They're still warm."

His eyes locked on hers. "Got to be another way out."

Running into a sitting room that adjoined the master bedroom, they found it, a rear door partially ajar.

Stephanie didn't wait another moment; she slammed through, Tate behind her. She heard him pull the door closed, but there was no way to lock it from the outside. Their pursuer would be right behind them.

She found herself running down a hallway that ended in a split stairwell. "Up or down?" she panted.

Tate pointed to a black scuff on the upper stair. "That way."

Both of them were breathing hard as they careened upward, finally coming to a door marked Roof.

"Wait," Tate called to her. "You don't know what's on the other side."

She didn't wait. She couldn't. Her father's life was on the line. She hurtled through and found herself on a flat rooftop, engulfed in a monstrous storm of noise. Wind whipped at her face and threw grit into her eyes.

She forced her head up anyway and saw a helicopter, rotors whirling.

The pilot in the cockpit gave her a startled look. In the back she could just make out a flash of silver hair—Wyatt Gage—and a familiar pale face beside him, an irritated Joshua Bittman.

The helicopter's engine whined, and it began to lift off.

"You can't take him!" she screamed over the roar. She took off running for the nearest landing skid.

"Steph!" Tate yelled. "No."

He made a grab for her, but she was too fast.

She increased speed and prepared to jump at the skid, which was now lifting off the ground.

Tate's fingers grazed her ankle and she lost her balance, rolling onto the cement roof, banging onto the hard surface, seeing in fleeting glances the helicopter well into the blue sky.

Getting to her feet, she ran to the edge of the roof, watching her father disappear. She whirled on Tate, tears streaming down her face. "You had no right."

"Would have gotten yourself killed," Tate said. His gray eyes were soft. "Your father wouldn't want you to risk it."

Fury, terror and grief rolled around inside, and she funneled them at Tate. "You shouldn't have done it!" she screamed. "You are not a part of my life anymore, Tate."

He flinched, but did not step back. "I know that."

She pressed her hand to her mouth to keep from shrieking, eyes drawn to her watch. Three fifty-nine. Thirty seconds until Bittman was supposed to have called. She'd blown it by coming here. She'd let her father down, let Victor down. She should have told Luca, let the cops know.

She struggled to breathe.

The door to the rooftop slammed open. The panting security guard stood there, gun drawn.

Tate raised his own hands and positioned himself in front of Stephanie. His face was hard, and she knew he'd lost, too—lost the chance to find his sister, if Bittman really was involved in her disappearance.

The man with the gun drew closer and she looked into the barrel, just as the phone in her pocket rang.

Tate watched the guard as indecision crept across his face. "No phones," he barked. "Get inside."

Stephanie nodded obediently and started toward the roof access.

Obedient? Stephanie? He tried and failed to recall a time when Stephanie genially obeyed a directive. Something was up, and he didn't have to wait long to see what she had in mind. She stopped suddenly, sucking in a breath. Pressing a hand to her side, she cried out, swaying until she went down on one knee.

The guard let down his gun arm as he reflexively moved toward her. Bingo. Tate dived, catching the guy in the solar plexus, tossing him backward onto the cement where he banged his head and blacked out. The gun spiraled out of his hand, and Stephanie kicked it to the corner. She was on her feet again in a moment, sprinting through the door and down the stairs.

"Wait, Steph," he called, to no effect.

Tate took a moment to remove the man's belt and use it to secure his hands behind him before he ran after her.

"What's the plan?"

"I'm going to the hospital, and then I'll find my father."

Tate saw the manic determination on her face. "The hospital? Tell me what's going on."

She didn't look at him, swiping her sheaf of dark hair

behind her ears. "Bittman wants something from me." She turned her face to his, and he saw for the first time the gleam of tears there. "He drove Victor off the road and took Dad. We don't know if Victor's going to make it."

"I'm sorry." Her brothers, though they held nothing but animosity toward him, were her entire world. For one crazy moment, he wanted to wrap her up in an embrace. "How does it fit together? What is Bittman after?"

"I can't tell you any more."

He folded his arms. "We've been through this already so cut out the dramatics. I want to know what's going on, and you're going to tell me."

Her eyes glittered. "I wasn't supposed to get anyone involved or he'll kill my father."

"Too late. I'm involved."

Her eyes grew cold. "No, you're not, Tate." With that she pushed by him, leaving a tantalizing whiff of the cinnamon fragrance she always wore.

He followed behind her as she exited the mansion, got into the pristine Mustang and roared out of the driveway. When the dust settled, he made his way back to the motorcycle, still hidden in the trees.

Why, he wondered, could he pass through his day without remembering so much as what he had for lunch, but he could minutely recall Stephanie's face after seeing her, even only briefly, for the first time in four years? It was so unfair, especially when every detail—the full lips, the electric brown eyes, the determined set to her chin—reminded him of his greatest failure. Pain rippled through him again.

*You are the worst thing that ever happened to Stephanie Gage.*

He shook away the thoughts. He'd come to find Maria, and instead he'd fallen into Stephanie's life and that of the man he despised above all others, Joshua Bittman. They'd met enough times years before when Stephanie started consulting for him. Tate pegged him as an arrogant, condescending egomaniac with more than a casual interest in Stephanie. It might have been coincidence that, after a heated encounter with Bittman, whom he'd thought was trying to win Stephanie's affections, his business contacts had dried up. Fuego Demolition suddenly had regular clients canceling contracts without notice. He'd never been able to prove it was Bittman, but it gave him even more reason to find his sister and make sure Bittman hadn't done something to her.

He flipped open his cell and punched in Gilly's number. Gilly was an eccentric computer whiz he'd known since the sixth grade. "Need a favor. Can you find out which hospital Victor Gage was transported to? Car accident."

"What's going down?"

"I'll let you know as soon as I do."

Gilly provided him with the answer in moments.

Not involved, Stephanie said? He threw a leg over the seat of the motorcycle in spite of the ripple of pain. Not likely.

Kicking the engine to life, he roared off the property.

Stephanie was not aware of the miles unrolling under the tires of her car. Her mind worked and reworked plan after plan as she hurtled toward the hospital. Each idea disintegrated into the anguished scream of her heart. *Daddy, Daddy.* She'd let Bittman take him. What had her father thought as he lifted off into the sky, looking down at the daughter who had failed to save him from a madman? Bile rose in her throat, and she fought the urge to floor the gas pedal, instead cutting around a driver in a van so closely that she could see his crew cut and the arch of his eyebrows. Tate had no right to interfere.

The call, the one at precisely four o'clock as she stared into the barrel of the security guard's gun, had been from

Bittman. She phoned him back with no answer. She knew the unspoken message.

*You didn't follow directions, Stephanie.*

*You told Tate Fuego.*

*Now your father will die.*

Tate's interference might have cost her father his life. She fought to control the spiraling panic.

*Focus, Steph. Figure out what to do.*

Bringing in the cops would seal her father's fate. He would be found dead with not one shred of evidence linking Bittman to the crime, just a few phone calls. No menacing messages saved to voice mail. No incriminating texts. No one in his employ would dare testify that her father had been imprisoned at his mansion.

The picture of innocence.

And Victor might not live to identify the car that ran him off the road, or the person who removed Wyatt Gage from the car. As she parked and entered the hospital, heading for the elevator, she was a mass of indecision. She had no idea what she would say to Luca to explain her absence. As soon as the elevator doors opened, Luca shot to his feet from the waiting room chair.

She hurried to him. "How is he?"

"Stable, for the moment. Brooke's on a plane." He folded his arms. "Where have you been? And don't sugarcoat it."

"I'm going to see Victor, then we'll talk." Luca's thick brows drew together, but he didn't stop her. Victor's room was small. One tiny window looked into the San Francisco sky. He lay in the bed, dark hair shaved on one side and head swathed in bandages. Bruises darkened his face, and an IV snaked out from under the blanket.

Her eyes filled with tears. "Oh, Victor. I'm so sorry." Bittman was a plague set loose on the Gage family because of her. As soon as she'd accepted Bittman's offer of full-time work, he'd believed he owned her, and now her brother was paying for that horrendous decision. Her throat closed up, aching with grief. "I wish you could tell me what to do."

"About what?" Luca leaned against the doorway.

She kissed Victor on the forehead and followed Luca back out to the empty waiting area. Staring into her brother's troubled green eyes made her stomach clench into a tighter knot. "Luca…" She trailed off. Would telling him result in another accident? She couldn't risk it. "It's nothing. I'm going to do a computer search…to see who might have wanted to hurt Victor."

"I'm not buying it. Where have you been?"

"At Bittman's," came a voice from the far side of the room. Stephanie's heart plummeted when Tate sauntered up.

Luca stiffened, hands balled into fists. "I should have known. Whatever trouble she's in concerns you."

"Not me. Bittman." Tate flicked a glance at her. "Tell him."

She glared back. "No, Tate."

"You don't have any choice, Steph," Tate said, eyes blazing. "You can't find him by yourself. Tell him, or I will."

Stephanie took a breath. Tate had backed her into a corner. Hands clenched, eyes on the floor, she told Luca everything. When she finally looked up, he was staring at her in disbelief. Then his eyes swiveled to Tate. "All right. This is family business, and we'll find a solution. Get out."

Tate shook his head. "Nope. My sister's disappeared, and Bittman has her or knows where she is. I'm staying until this plays out. Deal with it."

It happened in a flash. Luca had Tate by the shirt, and they went over in an angry pile of flying fists. Stephanie yelled and tried to grab Tate, but he wrenched away. Only a shout from an approaching police officer brought them to a standstill. The cop's name badge read Sergeant Rivers.

"What's going on here?" he demanded.

Luca and Tate got to their feet. Luca swiped at his forehead. "Sorry, officer. I lost my temper."

The officer looked from Luca to Tate. "That right?"

Tate nodded. "I egged him on. Wrong thing to do. Won't happen again."

He gave them another hard look before he turned to Luca. "I'm following up on our earlier conversation. I came by to tell you we've turned up nothing trying to ID the hit-and-run driver. How did you do coming up with any potential enemies?"

Stephanie caught Luca's eye. She sent him a pleading look and a shake of her head. Luca hesitated for an excruciating moment. "Nothing yet, but my sister's here now. We'll see if we can think of anything useful."

The officer's gaze flicked once more over the three of them. Then he nodded and excused himself to make a phone call.

Luca rounded on Tate. "Just so we're clear. You're no good for my sister, and you're not welcome here. You're involved only until we hand this over to the police or decide on a plan to get our father back."

"And my sister." Tate's lip curled. "You remember my sister, Maria, don't you Luca? You two have a history, don't forget."

Luca's face was a mask of rage. Stephanie stepped between them. "In light of the situation," she hissed, "can you two knock it off?" She felt the beginnings of an idea flash through her. "My files. I kept paper files when I worked for Bittman. Just odds and ends, bits that I found unusual in his business dealings. Maybe there's something in there that might give us a search direction."

She didn't want to go back to those dark days, the path she had taken that whisked her away from her family, from her faith. The twinges had been there when she first started doing some consulting for Bittman, a year before Tate's father was killed. Tate hadn't wanted her anywhere near Bittman. Tate's words rang in her mind.

*The way he looks at you...he wants you. You've got to quit working for him.*

She'd brushed him off, chalked up his reaction to jealousy. Maybe she was even the tiniest bit flattered by it. In any case, her stubborn streak would have prevented her from giving up a job she enjoyed. The work intrigued her, challenged her, but she'd felt the odd sense every now and again that something was not right.

God had been talking to her even then, but she hadn't listened.

Luca nodded, eyes riveted to hers. "It's the last effort before we go to the cops, Steph."

She was already heading for the door. "I'm going home to look."

He shifted uneasily. "I don't want you going alone."

She smiled. "I'll be okay. You need to stay here until Brooke arrives."

Luca checked his watch. "She should be here in a few hours. Then I'll come. Let me call someone to go with you."

"I'll go." Tate's tone was casual, but Stephanie could hear steely determination underneath.

"No way." Luca took a step toward her.

Tate hooked his thumbs through his belt loops. "Doesn't matter what you want."

"She'd be safer alone." Luca's green eyes shone with anger.

Stephanie didn't want Tate around any more than her brother did. She also knew that every moment they wasted brought them closer to disaster. She went to Luca and hugged him. "I'll be okay."

He squeezed her. "Don't let him back into your life," he whispered in her ear. "He's trouble."

*Trouble.* Truer words were never spoken. She kissed his cheek and headed for the door, trouble following right along behind her.

# THREE

Tate parked the motorcycle on the curb outside Stephanie's Victorian. She was already headed inside, the afternoon sun casting long September shadows over the neat yard, catching the gloss in her dark hair. The idiocy of his own actions came sharply home.

At worst, Stephanie despised him—and with good reason. He was, after all, a former drug addict who pushed her away, ignored her repeated attempts to get him help, and nearly ran her down while trapped in a cloud of painkillers. As for Luca, he'd just as soon take Tate apart one piece at a time. Not surprising. The Gages were tight and, in times of crises, impenetrable in their solidarity. They'd been just that way when he had descended into addiction. Guilt flared anew, along with the pain in his leg.

The Fuego family was an altogether different bunch, he thought with bitterness. They scraped for every opportunity, earned their living through hard work. Truth was, he'd been lost in a narcotic haze when his sister needed him the most, when she moved in with Bittman, six months after Stephanie quit working for him. Tate had been too addicted to painkillers prescribed after his leg was ruined in the accident that killed his father to do anything about it. Again the guilt stirred inside, but he fought it down.

His life had turned out scarily similar to his work as a demolitions expert. All the meticulous planning, endless mental rehearsal and the best of intentions was supposed to ensure that a condemned building would fall neatly, right on its footprint, with no overspray of deadly flying debris or partial failures that left structures tilting dangerously, still primed to explode. His relationship with Stephanie had turned out to be more like the time he'd witnessed the deadly power of a shock wave, a wave of energy and sound released when Fuego Demolitions took down a building. The massive wave traveled upward as was intended, before hitting a heavy cloud cover that forced the energy outward, exploding windows in the neighboring buildings. He could still hear the sounds of that shattering glass with the same perfect clarity that he recalled the end of his life with Stephanie.

He hesitated, trying again to steady his nerves. "Time to show some Fuego solidarity and do what you have to do to find Maria," he muttered to himself. It would be difficult because it meant sticking close to the most amazing woman he had ever known, a woman he could never have again, due to his own personal destruction.

*Forget about your past with Stephanie. Find Maria. That's all you've got left.*

He marched resolutely to the door and let himself into a small kitchen, painted in soft yellow tones. In the next room he could see boxes stacked in neat piles. "Nice place. Just moved in?"

"Couple days ago. I haven't made the time to unpack." She busied herself preparing coffee and pulling a plate of cheese from the refrigerator, along with a box of crackers, before she opened a can of cat food and put it on the floor. "Tootsie never misses a meal. She's like clockwork."

He watched her put the cheese and crackers on the table. "There's bottled water in the fridge."

"You don't have to feed me, Steph."

She adjusted the crackers in the bowl, removing three broken ones and tossing them in the trash. "It's going to take hours to go through the files. You'll be on your own."

"Is this your way of keeping me out of your hair?"

She looked at him then, eyes like melted chocolate. Suddenly she was the sixteen-year-old girl he'd met while running the track in high school, eyes sparkling as she challenged him to a race. His stomach jumped. For a moment he thought she would say something, but her expression changed and she headed for the front room. "My files are in here."

He sighed. Stay in the kitchen and be quiet, was the unspoken command. She ought to know that *idle* wasn't his natural state. The kitchen window framed a view of the street, quiet and empty except for a few parked cars, two Prius and another one. He leaned forward. The other was parked a good block away, a streamlined black Mercedes. Something about it struck a familiar chord.

As he turned it over in his mind, another thought occurred to him. "Steph?" He poked his head into the front room. "Where's the cat?"

"What?" she said, blinking at him, a file folder in her hands.

"The cat. You said she was like clockwork about her food." He gestured to the kitchen. "Hasn't been touched."

Stephanie's brow furrowed. "I'll bet she's stuck in the upstairs bedroom again. The door swings shut and she gets locked in."

"I'll check." He eyeballed the front door before he left and made sure it was locked. Probably nothing but his paranoia in action, but he doubled back and locked the kitchen door, too, before he made his way quietly across the hardwood floor and up the creaking stairs, which emptied out onto the long hallway, with three doorways. Two were open, the one on the far end, which Tate surmised was the extra bedroom, was closed. He walked slowly, scanning the two open rooms: a bathroom and another small room filled with more boxes. One more door beckoned. He approached slowly, put an ear to the wood and listened. No sound.

He felt slightly ridiculous prowling the property, but if Stephanie was right, Bittman had nearly killed Victor and taken her father. He wanted something from Stephanie, and he would no doubt do anything to get it. Tate told her flat-out when she started working for him that something wasn't right, but she'd laughed it off, accused him of being the jealous type.

Not jealous, just perceptive. Bittman was crazy, and she should have trusted Tate. He felt a flash of anger followed by another surge of guilt. Who was he to blame her for not trusting him? He'd proven later that he was not a man she could count on.

Tate put a hand on the knob and turned it, inch by inch, until the door released. Pushing it open, he scanned the inside. A small bed, neatly made. Another door leading to what must be a bathroom, and one more, a paneled closet. He started with the closet, rolling it open slowly. Empty, not so much as a forgotten coat. The stack of three boxes nearby indicated she'd not yet gotten around to the spare room. This was odd for Stephanie, who was manically organized, a woman who arranged her books on the shelves according to size and color. It was not like her to leave anything half done, even after only a few days in her new space.

A soft thump came from the bathroom. He froze, listening. Another thump and a soft scuffling noise. The cat? Maybe. Maybe not. He crept closer to the door, which was pulled mostly closed. Since he hadn't turned on the light, the room was dim. Easing along one footstep at a time, he hoped the squeak of the worn floorboards under his feet would not give him away.

Drawing close enough to see through, he caught the flutter of movement. He did a slow count to three and threw open the door. It crashed into the wall behind as he leaped through. A pigeon with iridescent feathers around its neck fluffed in alarm from its perch on the rim of the old-fashioned bath tub. With an irritated flap of feathers, it flew back to the window and scuttled through the gap.

He watched the pigeon disappear through the open window.

It took only a moment for him to notice the scuff mark on the sill, a black heel mark that could only have come from a man's shoe.

Stephanie shoved the papers into the folder in disgust. What did she hope to find? How could she win against Joshua Bittman when he held the ultimate card? Her father's life. She tried to take a calming breath and offer up a prayer, but her mind was too scattered. She had to figure out a way, without Tate's help. His lazy smile replayed itself in her memory. His sister was so like him, though neither one would admit to it, except for one important difference. Maria led with her emotions, her passions and disappointments written on her face for all the world to see.

Bittman saw that need in Maria and exploited it, no doubt, after Stephanie quit his employ and tried to remove him from her life. Futile effort. Everywhere she went, he kept tabs on her, reminding her in the subtlest ways that he remained in her life in spite of her feelings. Phone calls, texts, jewelry delivered to her various apartments, even the smell of his peculiar cologne wafting through her car told her he was close, so close, with unrestricted access to her.

And now, it seemed, to her family and Tate's. Stephanie

closed her eyes, thinking once again that the blame for Maria's relationship with Bittman lay squarely at Stephanie's feet. She did not believe, however, that Bittman had disposed of Maria in some violent manner. He didn't need to. With his wealth and enormous power, he could cut her out like a diseased patch of flesh. She would never get close to him unless he desired it. So Tate was wrong about the fact that Bittman made her disappear. If he would listen to reason, she could explain it to him.

Getting to her feet, she heard a soft meow from the room earmarked for a guest room if she ever managed to put down roots.

She pushed open the door, calling up the stairs as she did so. "I found her, Tate."

There was an answering shout from upstairs, but she did not respond, her attention riveted by the man sitting ramrod straight in her grandmother's old rocking chair.

"Hello, Stephanie," Bittman said, stroking the cat curled in his lap. "You look breathtaking."

The folder slipped from her fingers, papers floating to the floor around her feet. She wanted to scream, to yell to Tate, but nothing would come out of her mouth. Bittman eased the cat from his lap and brushed at a few hairs left on his pants. His face was smooth and unlined, approaching his mid-thirties. Long, dark hair combed away from his high forehead accentuated the pale skin, brown eyes glinting through small angled glasses.

He gestured to the bed. "Please, sit down. I imagine your oaf of a boyfriend will be here in a moment."

*He's not my boyfriend,* she wanted to whisper. Instead she took a deep breath, fighting down the fear that clawed at her throat, anger rising along with it. "I don't know what kind of sick game you're playing, but I want my father back right now."

Bittman chuckled, his glasses glinting in the dying sunlight. "Impatient as ever. I will hold off until Mr. Fuego makes it down the stairs."

They didn't wait more than a few seconds before Tate crashed through the door. His eyes sought hers, simmering with a mixture of anger and something else. "You okay?" he asked softly, pulling a phone from his pocket.

She nodded.

Bittman sighed. "Mr. Fuego, put away the phone. You will not be calling the police or anyone else. Stephanie doesn't want you to do that."

His lips quirked into a smile. As much as she wanted Tate to call the police, to have the supreme satisfaction of watching Joshua Bittman go through the demeaning process of being handcuffed on his way to jail, she knew the cost was too high.

"Put it away, Tate. I have to know what he wants from us."

"Where's my sister?" Tate demanded.

"I imagine this is why you intruded on my property."

"Where's Maria?"

Bittman's delicate eyebrows arched a fraction. "Mr. Fuego, you bore me. Running all over town like some Keystone Cop is not becoming. Stick with your current job. Blowing up buildings is more suited to your intellect."

Tate took a step forward. "Tell me."

Bittman gave him a cold stare. "Why would I tell you anything? You are, in the common vernacular, a loser. Addicted to painkillers, barely able to keep your father's business out of the red and, if my information is complete, the very same man who almost killed Stephanie, a woman who is far too good for you."

Stephanie's heart twisted, and she grabbed Tate's wrist before he could go after Bittman. "Just tell us what you want."

Bittman nodded. "Nothing from Mr. Fuego. His presence is strictly an annoyance, and I believe he went so far as to upset my birds, for which a price must be paid at some future date. They are blue mutation, yellow-naped Amazons—very rare, you understand." He gestured to the other wooden chair. "Please, sit down, Stephanie."

Stephanie remained standing, Tate next to her. "Where's my father?"

"Right to the point. No catching up?" His eyes swept over her body, making her face flush.

Tate grunted. "Get on with it."

Bittman ignored Tate. "Your father is fine for the moment, housed at a location which you will never find on your own until we conclude a business transaction. I need you to locate something for me, and once you do, he will be returned to you in mint condition. Simple as that."

Stephanie tried to read the feelings in his eyes, but failed. There was never any emotion to take note of, not in all the years she had known him. Only when he spoke of his own father did she see a spark. "What is it? This thing you need me to find?"

Bittman folded his arms and looked out the window, scrutinizing the view. "A violin."

"A violin?" Tate snapped. "You're loaded. Go buy your own."

Bittman kept his eyes on Stephanie. "This particular instrument was my father's. It was made in 1741. It is unique, virtually a living thing and it is worth, to put a crude price tag on it…"

"Eighteen million dollars," Stephanie said with a groan. "It's one of only a few made by an Italian craftsman named Guarneri del Gesu."

"How do you know that?" Tate asked.

"Because it was reportedly destroyed in a fire at Bittman's father's shop." Her stomach tightened. "I read about it."

Bittman's eyes flickered. "That information is incorrect.

The Guarneri was not burned, and I have recently acquired proof that it has surfaced right here in California. Someone has finally shown their hand by approaching a music store owner for repairs." His smile was terrifying. "I want my family's violin back. The person who possesses it can identify the arsonist who burned down my father's shop and killed my brother. I will be able to deliver the proper punishment, finally, after all these years."

Stephanie shivered. "There are plenty of other investigators and treasure hunters out there."

"I hired someone to gather information." His tone hardened. "Until that someone decided to go after my Guarneri herself."

Tate sucked in a breath. "My sister?"

Bittman glared. "Yes. It seems rotten apples are common on your family tree."

"Why would she want your violin? What did you do to her?"

"Nothing at all. I suspect the eighteen million dollars was motive enough."

Stephanie felt a sliver of fear for Maria. "Has she found it?"

"I am not certain. She took my research, a small matter as I have it electronically archived, of course. I'll get it back, and she will pay." The words had barely left Bittman's lips when Tate was on him, hands wrapped around his throat.

"You're not going to touch my sister," Tate barked.

Stephanie pulled Tate away, using all her strength to pry at his arms, which felt like steel bands under her fingers. "Let him go. You're not helping Maria." She had to keep Bittman talking long enough to find out how to rescue her father and now, it seemed, Maria, before Bittman got to her.

Bittman stood, adjusting his clothing. "I want you to locate my violin and the person in possession of it before Maria does. She might scare him off, and that would make me very angry, which, I am told, is a frightening prospect."

Tate's breath came in short bursts, and Stephanie worried for a moment that he would try to throttle Bittman again. She spoke quickly. "You could hire an investigator, a professional."

"But I want you, Stephanie. You have the Treasure Seekers' resources behind you and now, since your father's life hangs in the balance, you have the ultimate motivation to complete the mission for me."

Tate moved closer, and she felt his hand come to rest on the small of her back. It was the only thing that kept her mind from spinning completely out of control. For a moment, she thought Bittman was going to touch her, and she wondered how she would stand it. Tate tensed next to her, hand curled into a fist.

Bittman leaned close. "It is time for Treasure Seekers to go after the ultimate prize. Find it, and we will have everything we desire."

*We?* She pulled back slightly, her back pushed into Tate's chest. His fingers pressed her waist.

*I'm here. He's not going to hurt you,* the pressure seemed to say.

"And if I can't find the violin?" she whispered.

Bittman laughed softly before he whispered, "'I looked, and behold a pale horse...'" He gave her a smile that from anyone else would have been warm and filled with humor, but from him, held another meaning entirely. Icy trickles snaked up her spine in spite of Tate's reassuring touch and the fact that he moved her away from Bittman, inserting his own body between them.

Without a backward glance, Bittman was gone.

The room felt as if it was filled with tainted air, poisoned with a rank chemical that remained there even after Bittman's departure. She stumbled out of the room and back into the cheerful kitchen, which now brought no comfort.

Tate was speaking, but he had to repeat the question twice before it penetrated her haze of fear. "What's the business about the horse, Steph?"

She forced out the words. "We went riding a few times, back before I realized… He owns a stable full of the most beautiful horses you could imagine. So many to choose from, but he only rode one, a big stallion, completely white. The horse wasn't a good trail rider, too wild and headstrong. I asked him why he always chose that particular horse." She raised her eyes to Tate's. "He said he liked the imagery."

"Imagery?"

She swallowed hard. "It's from Revelation. 'I looked and behold a pale horse: and his name that sat on him…was Death.'"

# FOUR

Stephanie sat next to Luca on the flight to southern California. A few hours before, Victor's fiancée, Brooke, had arrived from San Diego to stay with Victor, who was showing signs of improvement. Stephanie offered up another prayer of thanks.

Luca did not want to leave their brother any more than she did, which added to the concern written on his face. They'd both thrown some necessities in a bag and she'd arranged for a neighbor to feed Tootsie before they were off to the airport. Luca was not one to rush anything, which she suspected added to his stress.

At least Tate was not with them to add fuel to Luca's ire. He'd stayed with her at her house, combing through the research that Bittman emailed just after he'd left, until Luca arrived sometime in the wee hours.

"Tate's not with Treasure Seekers. It's better that he stays out of our way," Luca growled.

"He's not going to. He thinks Bittman's going to hurt Maria, or she's going to do something dumb trying to get her hands on that violin. Either way he's going to stick with it until he knows for sure. He's meeting us at the airport in Bakersfield. From there we go to Devlin's shop. The one who contacted Bittman about the Guarneri."

Luca shook his head. "Tate will be a problem."

She allowed herself a smile, in spite of her weariness. "Dollars to donuts that's exactly what he's saying about you."

Luca did not return the smile. "Steph, he's bad news. Guy's a pill popper and a hothead."

Stephanie looked away for a moment. "I think he's clean now."

"You think?" Luca took her hand. "He almost got you killed. Plus, if he hadn't shut you out, treated you like dirt, you never would have taken such a tailspin and started working full time for Bittman."

She pulled away her hand. "Let's be clear. I joined Bittman of my own free will, tailspin or not. What's happening to Dad now, to Victor—" She blinked back a sudden onslaught of tears. "It's my fault, not Tate's."

He took her hand again, his expression softer. "No blame games here. I'm sorry. I get overprotective."

"You don't say."

He squeezed her fingers. "Just don't let Tate back into your life."

"Don't worry, I won't." *Once was more than enough.*

He relaxed. "Run me through it again, sis. Bittman's father owned a music store and he inherited the Guarneri from a deceased uncle some twenty years ago. The violin has some special name, doesn't it?"

"The Quinto Guarneri." She nodded, glad to be in problem-solving mode. "It was given that name by the virtuoso violinist who once played it. There was a fire and the Quinto was presumed destroyed, though Bittman claimed someone set the fire. He further claims a second person was in the shop, a homeless man Hans Bittman allowed to stay there. Bittman believes while he was trying to get his father, Hans, out, the homeless man made off with the Guarneri before the store burned to the ground, but the cops could not substantiate any of it. Bittman's older brother, Peter, was killed in the fire. He was mentally disabled; Bittman believes he hid under the bed until the smoke was too much for him. Hans Bittman went out of business and died shortly thereafter of a stroke."

Luca's eyes narrowed. "So Bittman thinks this violin that surfaced is the one stolen from his father and the guy who has it…"

She nodded. "Is the one who took it from the shop. He's also the guy who saw the arsonist and…" She trailed off.

"And what?"

"And it's the only time I ever saw him show emotion, the few moments when he spoke of his father or brother. Whatever happened that night changed him forever." She chewed a fingernail. "Bittman went to a lot of trouble to involve us."

Luca's eyes roved her face. "I think he's got ulterior motives. He wants you, Steph, that's clear. He's never gotten over the fact that you quit working for him."

Her cheeks flamed. "He had to know I would, after I found out that he used me to break into that security system." He'd directed her to steal a car, a Bugatti Veyron, supposedly to test out the antitheft system he'd installed. She'd stolen it all right, only it wasn't Bittman's car; it belonged to a man named Brown. The Gage family immediately rallied around Stephanie and appealed to Brown not to press charges. Brown was not swayed until suddenly, he dropped the charges with no explanation and sold the car to Bittman a week later. Stephanie had the suspicion Bittman had applied some excruciating pressure of his own. She also believed Bittman thought that by involving her in illegal dealings, he could blackmail her into staying with him. Blackmail was one of his specialties.

"You were more to him than an employee."

"Well, it wasn't mutual," she snapped. It was fun at first,

consulting for a man with a genius intellect, and then after Tate broke her heart, she desperately needed a distraction. Treasure Seekers was in its infancy with not enough projects to keep her busy, so she'd accepted Bittman's job offer to be his security consultant and design software protection systems. In all her time with Bittman, never did she feel any stirrings of love for the man. Bittman did not seem capable of love even if she had been interested, any more than a mountain cares for the clouds that surround it.

The flow of memories was interrupted by Luca's next question.

"Can you get a look at the police report?"

She shrugged. "I don't know. The local police department there was flooded about fifteen years back, so a lot of the records were destroyed."

His eyebrow arched. "But you're still working on it anyway, aren't you?"

"What makes you think so?"

He laughed. "It's like waving a steak in front of a hungry Doberman. You've got to know. It's what makes you a great Treasure Seeker."

She wanted to return the chuckle, but darker thoughts prevented her from doing so. *If I don't find this treasure, we might never see Dad again.*

The plane descended through an oppressive gray sky.

She wasn't surprised to find Tate waiting at the airport, sporting a neat T-shirt, a softly worn pair of Levi's and a baseball cap. He nodded at her and ignored Luca as they headed to the rental car counter.

"How's your brother?" Tate murmured into her ear, sending tingles dancing along her ribs.

"Stable for now. Did you fly?"

He shook his head. "Drove my friend's truck."

She started. "You didn't leave my place until almost one. You must have been driving all night."

He shrugged. "Don't sleep much anyway. Called my friend Gilly. He's gone to Maria's place. Checking her computer."

"Hacking into it?" Luca said.

Tate shot him a glance. "You worried about Maria's feelings? You didn't worry about those before."

Luca jerked to a stop and faced Tate. "I didn't touch your sister. Get that into your fat head."

"You saying she's a liar?" Both men topped six feet, and now they were nose to nose, anger simmering between them.

"Stop it," she hissed. "We have to work together."

"Doesn't mean I have to like it," Tate said.

Luca snorted. "Don't worry, none of us like it, so you're in good company."

Stephanie was relieved when Tate sat down to wait while Luca rented a car. She caught sight of a vending machine at the end of a quiet corner of the terminal. Stomach growling, she realized she could not recall the last time she'd eaten. Not wanting to take time to order from the café, she headed for the lone vending machine.

Away from the terminal noise, she shouldered her laptop strap and fished in her purse for loose bills, all the while wondering how she would keep Luca and Tate from killing each other long enough to find Maria or the violin. Her father would have told them both in that genteel way, "Cool heads, gentlemen." Thinking about him brought a lump to her throat. Had he been injured in the crash? Or worse? She only had Bittman's word that her father was unhurt. There had been bandages in the room where he had been held.

*God, please,* she whispered. *Please keep him safe until I find him.*

She felt off balance, useless, unable to locate her father

and not there for her ailing brother. On impulse, she pulled out her phone and dialed, surprised when Brooke answered.

For a moment she could hardly imagine what to say to this sweet woman who loved her brother so deeply. "It's Steph. I'm so sorry, Brooke."

"It's not your fault. Luca told me a little about what's going on, and you have to know this didn't happen because of you."

The words were kind, but they did not change the truth. "How is he?"

Brooke sighed. "Still unconscious, but the doctors are easing off the sedatives so if all goes well he should be coming around."

*If all goes well...*

"I'm glad you're there with him."

Brooke must have heard the unspoken feeling in her voice. "We both know you would be here, too, if you could. Just do what you have to do and stay safe. I'll stay right here with Victor, I promise."

Stephanie said goodbye and disconnected. What would happen when Victor did wake up? Would he remember the accident? Even more frightening, what if he was not himself anymore? What if he was damaged by the violence of the crash? The serious, steadfast brother whom she had relied on her entire life.

It was too much to worry about. Stepping around a man reading a newspaper, hat brim pulled down over his eyes, she continued to the machine.

Finally grasping some bills from inside her purse, she fed them into the slot. As her finger moved toward the button, the hair on the back of her neck stirred. Her subconscious knew someone was there before her ears detected the soft noise directly behind her. Before she could spin around, she was sandwiched against the machine by a man's heavy bulk, the breath forced out of her along with a cry. As she rallied to push him off, he jerked the laptop from her shoulder and ran down the darkened corridor.

She ran after him. He was strong and had the element of surprise, but she was fast and as determined as a lioness.

In a minute she'd caught up with him, his arms pumping as he headed toward the main terminal where she would lose him for sure. There was only one choice. With a surge of adrenaline, she leaped.

Tate was out of his chair as soon as he heard Stephanie's cry of surprise. He sprinted to the dim hallway in time to see a figure emerging with Stephanie's laptop under his arm. A moment later, Stephanie hurtled forward, catching the man by the ankles. They both fell, the man's hat flying through the air, along with the laptop. Tate ran to grab the man, but the assailant shook Stephanie loose with a vicious kick and leaped to his feet, running out the nearest exit door, grabbing his hat on the way.

Tate was paralyzed for a moment, wondering whether to pursue the laptop snatcher or help Stephanie. He decided on the latter. She was in a sitting position, blood oozing from the corner of her mouth, hair disheveled and cheeks pink with exertion.

He knelt next to her and a startled Luca joined them, along with an airport security officer who grilled them immediately.

"He tried to take my laptop," Stephanie puffed.

The security man answered a call from his radio. "No sign of the snatcher, but we'll keep looking." He gave her a quizzical stare. "I've been working here since the new terminal opened six years ago, and this has never happened before. Are you sure you don't know who that was?"

Stephanie shrugged. "He was wearing a hat."

"Uh-huh. Police will be here in a moment for your statement."

Tate and Luca helped her to a chair, and her brother gave her a tissue to apply to her lip. Another airport employee offered her medical attention, which she declined except for an ice pack.

"Are you sure you're okay?" Luca said.

She nodded. "Fine, just a bloody lip."

Tate shook his head. "You didn't think it would be nuts to try and tackle the guy?"

Her eyes opened wide in exasperation. "He tried to *steal* my *computer*."

Tate's stomach tightened as he looked at her, brown eyes glinting, outrage painted across her delicate features. Small woman, with courage as big as any man he'd ever met. He didn't love her anymore; there was too much anger and hurt between them to ever allow those feelings to take hold again. Still, he wondered why his heart beat unsteadily as he drank her in.

Luca sighed. "It won't do any good to tell her it was a dumb thing to do."

"Wasn't going to try."

Luca and Tate exchanged a look, probably their first that wasn't a hostile stare down.

"I'll go finish with the rental car then." Luca looked at Stephanie. "Can you just sit there until I get back?"

"I'll try," Stephanie said.

Tate reached over and picked a sliver of paper from her hair, smoothing the dark silky strands into place. Soft and fine, just like he remembered.

She pulled back and finger combed her hair into some semblance of order. "I'm sure I look ridiculous after rolling around the airport floor."

"Nope. Same as always. Raindrops on roses." As the

words left his mouth, his face flushed hot. Had he really said that? His mother always maintained that the most beautiful thing she could think of was raindrops on roses, and when he and Stephanie were together, it was his favorite way to tell her in his clumsy fashion how gorgeous she was. Gorgeous, perfect, different…and not his anymore. They were strangers, now and forever. He felt her eyes searching his face as he turned away, awkward as a teen boy.

He moved aside, pretending to look over the crowd, but inside blood pounded an erratic rhythm in his veins. *Go, do something, anything.* He pulled out his phone to check for messages he knew weren't there, then he strolled to the drinking fountain and sucked down some water. When he looked back again, he was relieved to see Stephanie deep in conversation with Luca. The slip hadn't meant anything to her. Nothing at all.

The cops arrived to take her statement. She didn't give them much. They were traveling on business; the would-be thief was a stranger. She provided a number where they could call with any follow-up questions, and that was that.

Luca and Stephanie retrieved their bags, and the three headed outside into the hot southern California air to pick up their rental car. Tate arranged to follow in the truck he'd borrowed from Gilly. After only a few paces, however, Stephanie stopped them both.

"I just figured it out."

"What?" both men said at once.

"The guy who tried to take my laptop."

"You said he was a stranger," Luca said.

"He is, but I've seen him before." Her dark eyes danced in thought. "I remember cutting around his van in traffic." She looked at Tate. "When we left Bittman's mansion, right after he flew off with Dad."

Tate's eyes widened. "I thought he seemed familiar." He

snapped his fingers. "The hair. It was Bittman's pool guy. He followed you from San Francisco."

"Who is he?" Luca grimaced in thought. "Someone Bittman hired to keep tabs on us?"

Tate shook his head. "Seems like he wouldn't have his flunkies interfere. What good would that do? His pool guy might be working against him."

"Why?" Stephanie's expression was grave. "Who even knows the violin still exists?"

Luca's face was grave. "Is it possible Bittman was right about what happened all those years ago at his father's shop? About the arsonist?"

"Not just an arsonist," Tate said. "Remember, the fire killed Bittman's brother."

"He's returned and he's after the violin. The person who has it might be able to finger him for murder. He wanted my laptop to see if we'd found anything that could help him." Stephanie felt her pulse pound. "I think we'd better get moving."

Tate was already on his way to the truck. "I think you're right."

# FIVE

Two hours after leaving Bakersfield, Tate guided the truck behind the rented Ford into a nearly empty parking lot, which served the music store and a sandwich shop in the minuscule town of Lone Ridge. The heat pressed in on them, making the asphalt shimmer in spite of the early fall color he detected on a few of the twisted trees. Tate wondered idly how Luca, who owned a car worth more than the trailer Tate lived in, felt about driving a regular vehicle. It was good for him to come down from his rich man's tower once in a while. *Might be a refreshing change,* he thought bitterly.

He shifted uneasily on the hard seat. Was that what had attracted Stephanie to him? He was a country boy who ate grits and drove a dinged motorcycle. Was he a diversion for her? A form of rebellion against her upper-crust family?

He rubbed at a spot on his jeans. He'd seen rebellion first-hand in Maria, becoming completely unmanageable when she turned eighteen, and then worse after their father died. The truth pricked at him.

*How would you know, Tate? You were so strung out on painkillers, you did nothing to rein her in.* He yanked open the door and plunged into the heat. Time for that to change.

Luca led the way into Devlin Music and Repair shop. The interior smelled musty, every square inch crammed with saxophones, trumpets, bins of neatly filed music and packages of reeds and guitar picks, old photos plastered to the walls with yellowing tape.

"We're here to see Mr. Devlin," Luca said to the short man who appeared at the counter. He was round and florid-faced, wearing a short-sleeved plaid shirt tucked into neatly creased pants. Around his neck hung a pair of reading glasses fastened to a brown cord.

Devlin looked closely at the three of them. "I'm Bruno Devlin. What can I do for you?"

Stephanie flashed a brilliant smile. "We're looking for an instrument—a very special instrument—and we were told you might have a lead on where we can find it."

Devlin's eyes narrowed a fraction. "You're not from around here." A German accent clung to his words.

"No, we came from San Francisco," she continued. "The instrument is a rare violin, a Guarneri."

His mouth opened and closed. "A Guarneri?" He choked out a laugh. "Here? In this nowhere town? I am afraid you have the wrong information."

Luca frowned. "I don't think so. Our facts came from a reliable source. I think you probably know him."

Devlin's Adam's apple jerked. His response came in a low tone. "Joshua Bittman sent you, didn't he?"

Stephanie nodded. "You contacted him and told him that someone had been in your shop, looking for some repair advice."

He looked at his glass counter and buffed at a spot. "Yes."

"Why deny it?"

"Please," Devlin said, wiping at his forehead. "I don't know what is going on. I called Mr. Bittman because he contacted every music repair store in southern California asking for any information on a rare violin. I did what he asked as a courtesy, and that's that. Just business. I don't know where the violin is."

Tate shook his head. "It's more than business. You knew Bittman's father." Stephanie and Luca started slightly at Tate's statement, as if they'd forgotten he'd been standing there.

"I..." the man started.

Tate pointed to an old yellowed photo on the wall, a smiling Devlin outside a shop sporting a sign that read Feather Glen Music, with the year scrawled in marker on the corner. "Feather Glen's in New York." He looked at Stephanie. "In your files you said Bittman's father owned a music shop in New York around that time, not too far from Feather Glen. The instrument repair business is a pretty small world." He looked at Devlin. "You must have known Bittman's father."

Devlin scratched at his chin. "Yes, I knew Hans Bittman. Our families were neighbors in Germany once. We spoke from time to time. He allowed me to come and see the Guarneri after he inherited it." Devlin's eyes shone. "Never have I seen such an instrument. People say the Guarneris are second to Stradivaris, but it is not so. The sound is darker, more intense, and it would take years to master one, perhaps a lifetime."

Stephanie pulled the conversation back on track. "So you saw the Guarneri?"

Devlin sighed deeply. "Yes, the very day before the fire. Tragic, tragic. I helped him try to salvage his business after, but it was no use. He was ruined, his eldest son dead. His other son, Joshua, he became a different person then, too. Something switched off inside him when his brother perished in that fire. Something...died." Devlin pointed to his chest. "He went a little crazy. He always claimed that a thief made off with the violin and another man set the fire."

"Do you think he was telling the truth about that night?"

He shrugged. "He was a child, and he believed what he thought he saw. Maybe it was one of the bums Hans took in from time to time. He was a soft man, let them sleep in the workshop and fed them sometimes. One of them probably snatched it, and the fire started accidently. Maybe Joshua made up the story in his mind to make sense of his brother's death and the loss of his father's beloved Guarneri. No one will ever know."

Tate saw Stephanie puzzling it over. "So you told Mr. Bittman that someone came in with a Guarneri. Who was it?"

Devlin shrugged. "A wild man. Crazy hair and beard. He brought only a picture of the Guarneri, an old-fashioned Polaroid."

"Do you still have the picture?" Luca asked.

"No, but he said he would send me another so I could get a replacement string. He said he would return, but he did not say when."

Luca leaned forward. "Where did he live? Around here?"

Devlin shrugged. "In the desert, a town called Bitter Song."

"Sounds like a real tourist mecca," Tate mumbled.

"It's in the Mojave," Devlin said with a shake of his head. "No sane person would want to go there."

Stephanie gave Devlin a card and instructed him to call if the stranger returned. Devlin did not touch the card, but left it on the counter.

"Mr. Devlin, can I ask you one more question?" Stephanie said. "Has anyone else been here asking about the violin? A man with a crew cut or a dark-haired girl?"

"No, no one."

She pressed her palms to the countertop. "Then who are you afraid of?"

He blinked. "Afraid? Why would I be afraid? Mr. Bittman

wants his violin, and I am helping him get it. You'll tell him, won't you? That I am helping him? Only him?"

Devlin didn't wait for an answer, but scurried away into the back room.

Stephanie stood staring after him. "*Only* Bittman? Do you think the pool guy or Maria beat us here and Devlin doesn't want to tell us?"

Tate's pulse quickened. "Let's ask some more questions around town. Maybe someone else will be more cooperative."

"And then—" Luca sighed "—we're headed to the Mojave."

"The place where only crazy people go," Tate finished.

"Then we'll fit right in," Stephanie said, leading the way back outside. "By the way." She pressed Tate's shoulder. "That was pretty good detective work in there, with the photo."

He shrugged, her fingers warm through his T-shirt sleeve. "Just trying to keep up with the real treasure hunters."

Luca gave him a quick nod of approval. "We would have come up with that eventually, but you saved us some time."

Tate put a hand to his baseball cap. "Anything to help."

She smiled, but beneath the expression he saw the deep current of fatigue, and something else…fear.

He flashed back to his own feelings the moment he'd woken up in the hospital and asked about his father after the car accident that took his life. Was the terror still etched deep inside his own eyes? he wondered. One moment had been rich with laughter and teasing.

*"When you gonna seal the deal and propose to that Stephanie gal? She needs a real man in her life."*

He remembered his father's hand, thick and callused, waving out the window of the truck as Tate followed in a second vehicle until the unthinkable happened. Before Tate's unbelieving eyes, his father suddenly careened over the side of a cliff. After a moment of frozen shock, Tate was out of his car, panic propelling him down the slope. Flames spurted from the wreck.

*I'm coming, Dad. I'm coming.*

But he was still fifteen feet away when there was a boom that shook the ground. He could not get out of the way as a hurtling piece of metal barreled at him with missilelike intensity. There was a sense of something slicing through his leg, the feel of bone snapping and then…darkness.

The darkness had not gone away when he came to. In fact, it seemed to have burrowed deep down inside him, awakening pain so excruciating he'd believed the pills were the only solution. His own weakness disgusted him. He was sure, even though he was no longer the same person he'd been, that his weakness disgusted Stephanie, too.

"Tate?"

He blinked back to the present. "So what's the next step?"

Luca pointed to a small café, fronted in sun-parched wood. "I'm going to go there, ask around. I want to run Mr. Devlin through our computers and see what comes up, and give Tuney a call."

Stephanie explained that Tuney was a private investigator who had helped them find Brooke's missing painting. "We're going to have him look for Dad." Her voice trembled a tiny bit until she cleared her throat.

"Tuney's not conventional, but he's more tenacious than anybody I've ever met. If anyone can find a crack in Bittman's plan, it's him. Steph, see if you can find out if Maria's been sighted around here," Luca said.

"So what am I supposed to do while the Treasure Seekers are hard at work?" Tate asked.

Luca marched across the street. "Poke around," he fired over his shoulder. "Check in with your source and see if anything's turned up on Maria's computer."

Tate scanned the street, a wide swath of worn asphalt, bordered by a few storefronts standing on either side, interrupted by flat stretches of dusty ground and piñon junipers. The mountains rose in the distance, giving Tate an uncomfortable, hemmed-in feeling. The street was completely deserted. Not a soul to be seen anywhere. He sighed. "Poke around, huh?"

Stephanie shouldered her laptop. "Luca is focused. He knows how to follow a trail. That's what we do."

He didn't answer. His leg was stiff from the long drive, a dull ache throbbing above the knee.

"We're going to find Maria," she added.

The token effort goaded him. He rounded on her. "So you're concerned now? Why did you let her hook up with Bittman in the first place? If you were trying to punish me, you did a great job of it." It wasn't fair and he knew it, but there was no taking it back now.

She glared at him. "I introduced them before I realized what kind of a man he was. Then I tried to steer her away from him, Tate. I did everything I could."

"You knew the truth about Bittman. Maria was just a kid. You didn't try hard enough."

Fire sparked in her eyes. "I'm no substitute for her big brother, and you weren't around. You can't blame me for that."

He wanted to snap off an angry reply, to meet her challenge with one of his own, but he found there was nothing to say. He turned away, determined not to limp.

"Tate, hold on," she called after him, voice contrite. "I know you had your own problems."

The shame burned through his good sense. He'd take her anger, her disgust, any emotion at all, but not pity. He stopped and spoke to his boots. "I took pills, Steph. Let's not soften it."

Her voice was soft. "You were in pain."

"Stop it." He whirled on her. "You don't need to make excuses for me. I'm clean now. I don't need your pity."

Her expression hardened. The gentleness in her eyes filmed over with something rougher. "You don't need me at all. You never did. You made that clear when you shut me out." She folded her arms across her chest. "I could have helped. That's what people do when they really love each other."

The words hung heavy between them. "I…" He ran a hand through his hair. "I'm going to check around."

Pain rippled through his leg, circling like a biting dog, along with more severe discomfort of another kind. He was wrong to blame Stephanie for Maria's predicament. Wrong. Shamed. Furious.

He pushed himself faster.

Ahead was the gas station, a run-down place sporting two pumps and a banged-up soda machine. Fighting to keep his mind off the conversation he'd just mangled, he passed a narrow alley between an empty warehouse and a storage locker facility. So lost in his own thoughts, Tate almost missed the muffled sound coming from the darkened alley.

Stephanie stalked back to the restaurant, her stomach in a tight ball of anger. When she forced herself to take some deep breaths, she realized she was furious with herself. Tate was history—whatever past they'd had was lost under a pile of disappointment and hurt. He was weak, because of the addiction he'd fallen into and his inability to accept the blame for his own failure toward Maria.

"Weak," she grunted to herself. She allowed herself a look back to confirm it, but her eyes saw something different than her brain. His wide shoulders were silhouetted by golden sunlight, head bent as if under some heavy burden. His limp somehow made him even more alluring. She exhaled loudly, certain that her mind was succumbing to pressure and worry. *Nuts, Steph. You're losing it completely.*

She slammed open the diner door so hard that the three patrons looked up in surprise. The waitress was the only one who did not look nonplussed. She smiled, her lipstick feathered slightly in the tiny lines around her mouth. "Table, miss?"

Stephanie pointed to her brother. Head ducked, she scurried to Luca.

"You look like you're ready to take on the world heavyweight champion. What's wrong? Did that idiot push your buttons?"

"He's not an idiot, Luca. He's a stubborn cowboy with a chip on his shoulder who wouldn't know a diamond from a doorknob, but he's not an idiot."

Luca blinked, smile held in check. "Whatever you say."

The waitress arrived, tucking a strand of silvered hair behind her ears. "Can I take your order, folks?"

Luca asked for a refill on his coffee.

"What kind of pie do you have?" Stephanie asked.

"Chocolate cream, banana, apple…" the woman recited.

"Whatever has the most chocolate in it, and make it a big slice," Stephanie said.

Luca waited until the waitress left. "I checked in on Victor. He's still stable, no change to report really."

Stephanie sighed, uncertain whether to be encouraged or disappointed at the news. "Tuney?"

"He's on board. He's going to work the helicopter angle, see if he can figure out where Bittman might have taken Dad."

She swallowed. "Do you think he'll be able to get a lead?"

"He's checking into the medical aspect, too, to see if Bittman hired a private nurse or doctor."

She tried to breathe out her terror. Tuney was a gruff character, crabby and volatile on the outside, but she knew him to be loyal, and most important, he understood what it was like to lose someone. "Good." She opened her laptop. "I'll keep working on the police report from Hans Bittman's store." It brought a surge of relief to be doing something. *One step closer to Dad,* she thought. She put her cell phone on the table. The waitress brought her a slice of pie that made her mouth water in spite of the mangled state of her nerves.

The laptop hadn't finished booting up when her phone vibrated with an unknown number. The hospital? She answered.

"Good afternoon, Stephanie."

Her breath froze in her lungs. "What do you want?"

Bittman laughed. "Is it unusual for a man to call and check on the progress of his employee?"

"We're not your employees, and we'll give you a report when we have some news," she hissed.

Luca gestured angrily for her to hand him the phone.

She mouthed the word *no*. Bittman did not want to talk to Luca; she knew that much.

"You've made contact with Devlin?" Bittman asked.

"Yes, and he's given us some info."

"Excellent. I'm confident that you will not have any interaction with the local police. They will only slow things down. No police whatsoever. That is clear, is it not?"

"Yes."

"Good. I have an update for you. It seems as though your father is determined to shed a few pounds."

She clutched at the phone. "What? What's wrong with him?"

"Nothing at the moment, but he is rejecting any food, even though we have provided him with some tantalizing fare. Ethnic food, I recall you said he enjoyed. Chicken mole?

Prepared with the most exquisite care, and yet he refuses to touch it. He has not become a vegetarian recently, has he?"

Her head swam. He was not eating. That meant surely he was growing weaker with every passing minute. "You've got to let him go."

Luca was on his feet now, grabbing for the phone, but she fended him off.

"No, I'm afraid that would not work out well. He's very irate and stubborn, as are the rest of the Gages. If you don't want him to continue to starve himself, you need to retrieve my violin and the person who possesses it quickly."

"We will." Stephanie fought to keep both rage and panic out of her voice. "Let me talk to my dad. Just for a minute. Surely that won't hurt anything? I've got to speak to him."

"Perhaps another time."

"No, please." She hated the pleading note in her voice. "I…" She swallowed. "I would really appreciate it."

Bittman laughed. "Oh, Stephanie. A conciliatory tone does not win you any points with me. I admire you the way you are, fiery and totally unapologetic."

She gritted her teeth. "Let me talk to my father."

"Not right now, Stephanie. You have a violin to find," he laughed softly, "and a lovely slice of pie to enjoy. Goodbye."

Stephanie sat frozen, phone in her hand, staring down at the fat wedge of chocolate pie waiting for her on the scratched diner table.

# SIX

Tate had the sensation of being watched as he sauntered along the sidewalk. Striving to keep his gait casual, shoulders relaxed, he walked by the alley, littered with stacks of boxes, the end concealed by a rust-blackened Dumpster. After a few paces he turned around, in time to see a figure ducking into the alley to escape detection.

Tate made his way as quietly as he could down the passage, passing by garish graffiti, trying to avoid breathing in the stench of rotting garbage. He stopped near where he was sure the man was hiding. "Come on out. Face me like a man," he called.

A figure stepped from the shadows. It was the man from the airport, the one who'd tried to grab Stephanie's laptop, the one who had driven the pool van onto Bittman's property. His graying crew cut glistened with sweat.

Tate looked him over. "Who are you?"

The older man raised an eyebrow. "Who are you?"

"All right. I'll play. I'm Tate Fuego. What do you want with Stephanie Gage? I know you tried to take her laptop at the airport, and now you're following me. Why?"

He opened his mouth, eyes wide with surprise before they narrowed into slits. "I don't know what you're talking about."

"Yes, you do. You were working as the pool guy at Joshua

Bittman's estate, and now here you are. How do you explain that?"

He smiled, showing yellow teeth. "Coincidence."

"I don't think so. Since you were hanging around Bittman's, you might have seen my sister, Maria. I'm looking for her." Tate saw no flicker of recognition cross the man's face. "Do you know where she is?"

"I don't know any Maria."

"What about Bittman? You're his pool guy, but something tells me you weren't just there to fix the chlorine."

"You're mistaken."

The lie ignited a slow burn in Tate's chest. "Know what I think?" He held his hands loose at his sides, ready. Considering the older man's crooked nose and battle-hardened face, he figured the guy would read the signs. He was right.

The man eased himself into position, ready for a fight. "What's that, boy?"

"I think you're a liar. I think you're going to tell me why you're here, what you want with Stephanie Gage and what you know about my sister."

The man's hands balled into fists, instead of reaching behind him to his waistband. Tate felt relief. Fists he could handle—but a gun? Not so easily.

"Could be you're wrong about that," the man said.

Tate shifted his weight forward. "Maybe, but you're not leaving this alley until I find out why you're here."

The man dived at him, moving with surprising quickness. Tate managed to step to the side, but it didn't throw off the attack for long. The punches came in rapid succession, and took all Tate's powers of concentration to block them.

He ducked an incoming blow, which infuriated the attacker, who staggered as his punch fell short, glancing off Tate's shoulder. Tate used the moment to deal the man a violent shove to the side, sending him sprawling into a pile of plastic trash bags disgorged from the overflowing Dumpster.

Fighter that he was, the guy was on his feet again in seconds.

"How about you tell me your name?" Tate said, fists up and ready. "Since we're getting along so well and all."

A hint of a smile twisted his mouth. "Name is Ricardo, boy."

"I didn't catch your last name."

Again the smile. "Feel free to make one up."

"Are you here on Bittman's dime? Keeping tabs on us, maybe?" The eyes sparked, but Tate could not read an answer in the grim expression. A scent of cigarettes clung to the man.

A shout from the end of the alley drew both their attention. Before he realized what was happening, Ricardo dived behind the Dumpster and scrambled up a worn ladder that Tate hadn't even noticed bolted to the side of the building.

Tate followed, kicking aside bags of trash until he grabbed hold of the iron rungs. "I've seen this in movies," he called up. "It's no good climbing to the roof unless you've got a helicopter waiting for you."

Climbing was agony on his leg, but he forced himself upward, burning with shame that a man twenty years his senior could climb twice as fast. Teeth gritted, he continued, sparing only a quick look at the alley below.

Figures darted in and out of the shadows. One could have been Stephanie. He was glad he'd encountered Ricardo before Stephanie did because he knew from the kickboxing class they'd taken that she was a fierce combatant. She'd take Ricardo on in a heartbeat, especially after he'd tried to steal her laptop. He smiled, in spite of the fire in his thigh. Five feet to go before he crested the top. Ricardo might be waiting there for him. One good kick in the head, and Tate would find himself back in the alley the hard way. He pressed on, hands raw from the abrasion of the rough metal.

He stopped, head ducked two rungs before the top. He heard footsteps, but not close. Heaving himself up and over, he rolled immediately to the side and scrambled behind the nearest cover, a metal vent.

Ricardo was running toward the other side of the rooftop. Tate ran after him, catching up just as Ricardo came within a few feet of the ledge. Tate's heart pounded. The gap between the building and the lower storage unit next to it was no more than six feet, but the drop was a good twenty. It might not kill a man, if he landed feet first—but then again, it might.

Ricardo eyed the gap, and then Tate.

"This time I can read your mind, boy," Ricardo said, voice low. "You think an old man cannot make this jump."

"Not exactly," Tate said, edging closer. "I think an old man would be crazy to try it."

Ricardo smiled. "And I think a man with a crippled leg would be equally loco to consider it, eh?"

Tate kept his face neutral. "We can talk. Work together."

He didn't answer. Before Tate could react, Ricardo sprinted to the edge of the building and hurtled over the side.

Stephanie raced up the ladder as soon as she saw Tate following the crew-cut guy to the top. She had to get to the roof to help him.

Her fingers were still trembling from the phone call.

*You have a lovely slice of pie to enjoy.*

Had she been so naive as to think Bittman would let her wander off to find his treasure unsupervised? Was he even now watching her through some long-distance lens, tracking her every step? Paying the waitress to report back to him? And, she thought grimly, taunting her with the fact that her father was refusing to eat.

*Another game. Showing you he owns you, controls you. He has all the power.*

With a sick feeling, she realized that he did, in fact, hold all the power. What could she do except find his violin and hope he would keep his word to return her father? It was like trusting a cobra not to strike.

She pushed herself to the top, emerging onto a flat cement roof that shimmered in the heat. A blur of movement told her the crew-cut man had just leaped from that very rooftop. She read Tate's body language as he backed up, though she didn't believe what her brain was telling her. He was going to do the same—leap off the roof to the building next door.

"Tate!" Her voice came out in a shriek.

He started and turned. "It's the guy from the airport. Tell you later." He tensed to begin his sprint.

"Stop right there. You're not jumping."

He cocked his head. "I can make it."

"No, you can't, not with your leg." It was the wrong thing to say. Stubborn lines appeared around his mouth.

"I can do it."

She took a step closer and tried for a calm tone as she pulled out her phone. "Luca's down there. I'll text him." Her thumbs flew over the keys, though she didn't take her eyes off Tate.

Tate looked toward the edge, eyes calculating the distance.

Her instincts demanded that she yell, grab hold of his ankles if she must and keep him from jumping, but the truth was that Tate could not be forced—nor coerced—into anything. She took a breath, entreating God to help her find the right words. "I'm asking you not to do that, Tate. Please."

He cocked his head, eyes bright with surprise at her change in tone. "Why?"

*Why?* Common sense, of course. If Tate was injured it would slow them down, add to the difficulties they were already facing. Purely a practical reason, a counter to his irrational notion. She looked away from his intense gaze. "Because my brother is hurt, my father is missing and I can't take anything else." She hated the way her voice broke. Her words betrayed an emotion that she would not voluntarily bare to Tate Fuego at any price.

He looked at her for what seemed like forever, though it was probably only a moment. Then his gaze slid back to the gap, and she knew that he was going to jump. He turned to the edge.

He was a hopelessly stubborn man who would run to his own destruction. She closed her eyes and imagined what it would be like when he was gone, too. Pain drove the breath from her.

When she opened her eyes, he was still there, only now he was close. So close he reached out a hand and eased the tears from her cheeks, tears she had not even known were falling. His face was tender, younger, the same face that she saw in her sweetest dreams before reality cruelly imposed itself. There was an odd questioning look there, too.

She let herself feel the gentle caress before she pulled away and angrily wiped her face. "I'm getting weak."

He chuckled, the remnants of the quizzical look still playing about his lips. "No, ma'am. Still the strongest Gage I know. Let's go see if your brother managed to accomplish anything."

She climbed down first, which allowed her time to grab hold of her fraying emotions. Crazy—she was becoming crazy. The longer this horrendous treasure hunt ensued, the closer she edged to complete insanity.

Luca was there the instant she touched ground. "I found his car at the other end of the alley. He took off."

"You didn't stop him?"

Luca smiled. "As a matter of fact, I let him go."

Tate exploded, limping up to Luca as soon as he touched ground. "What? Why would you do that? What kind of game are you playing?"

Luca waved him off. "No game, just a tracking device I stuck to his car."

Tate did not relax. "We should have questioned him first, found out what the deal is with him and Bittman."

"Could be he's working for Bittman as some extra insurance in case we don't complete the job, but that doesn't explain why he went for Stephanie's laptop."

"Or he's the one who killed Peter, and he's going to try and get his hands on the violin and its current owner," Stephanie mused.

"All we've got are guesses," Tate snarled. "You're taking risks with my sister's life."

"We've got a life involved in this, too, Fuego, in case you've forgotten," Luca said.

Their loud exchange was drawing attention from the gas station attendant, who had emerged from his tiny office.

"Quiet, both of you," Stephanie said. "Let's get out of here before the police come around." Thinking of Bittman's earlier message made her shiver. It also reminded her that time was ticking away. She pushed them both toward the car. "I'm riding with Tate. I want to know exactly what the guy said to him. We'll follow after you get a GPS signal."

Without waiting for his reply, she jumped into the passenger seat of Tate's truck. All business. No need to talk about her strange reaction on the roof.

"Get this relic started before Luca takes off without us." She felt eyes on her, Bittman's eyes, watching as Tate related the encounter with Ricardo. He gave her a strange look but eased the truck out onto the road after Luca's rental car.

"What happened that I don't know about?"

With a sigh, she told him about the phone call in the restaurant. He stared at her. "He's got tabs on you down here? What exactly is Bittman capable of?"

Stephanie wanted to close her eyes and avoid the question, but she could not. "Anything." She saw the muscles work in his jaw. "I finally realized that, when he used me to steal that car. I would have left anyway because it was becoming clear to me how he made his money."

Tate quirked an eyebrow. "I thought he was into communications systems."

"He creates billing systems, phone and internet, for big companies, only he tacks on a small charge to each bill, a few pennies in some cases. The surplus is routed to his accounts. The amounts are so small that they go undetected, and he makes millions. It's called salami slicing."

"You didn't go to the police?"

"I didn't have proof. Only suspicions and…"

"And?"

"And the day after I resigned, he sent me a photo."

"Of what?"

"My brothers and me at a family party, a private party in my father's backyard. I don't know how he got the picture."

Tate's mouth tightened. "Guy's got millions. He can buy whatever he wants."

"Not everything."

Tate was eyeing her closely. "So this is not just about the violin, is it?"

"He's…he's tried to get me back into his life. Everywhere I've gone, he's followed. Made phone calls, sent flowers." She swallowed. "Once I got home to find my neighbor had moved out suddenly. He was a nice man, a college student who used to bring me vegetables from the farmer's market." She looked out the window at the dust blowing along the side of the road. "To say Bittman's jealous is an understatement. He never liked it when I mentioned you as a matter of fact, back when I was just consulting for him. He said he'd known you weren't good for me. Made me think he'd been watching me for some time."

She'd had her proof later, after she'd left Bittman's employ. It came in the form of a photo Bittman had sent, a picture of Tate entering a church-run drug counseling clinic. He looked terrible, worn out, cheek bruised by a fall, she'd guessed, eyes bloodshot and miserable. Her heart had broken all over again when she saw that photo.

Though it hadn't included a note, Bittman's message was clear.

*You see? A loser, just like I told you.*

"Did you have feelings for him?" His tone was sharp as glass.

She bridled. "That's not your business, Tate, but no. He was strictly an employer in my mind."

"You could have worked anywhere. Why work for him?"

*Why him? Because he was interesting and smart and he distracted me from thinking about the man I really loved, the man who pushed me out of his life.* "You don't get to interrogate me," she said, voice bitter.

Tate blew out a breath. "I told you when you first started consulting for him that he was a freak. You're smart and you're well connected. How could you ever have let that guy into your life?"

"Maybe because I don't like being told what to do. Your sister fell in with Bittman, too, remember?"

"Different story. My sister has always fallen for the wrong guy. She was impressed with his money, I'm sure, flattered to be hired by him to do his odd jobs. Never bothered to look deeper than the car and the fancy house."

"Maybe she just wanted someone to listen to her."

"I listened."

"No, you lectured." She sighed. "And so did I. I told her

everything, but all she knew was that he showed interest in her."

His eyes flicked to her face and quickly away. "And I didn't."

She didn't answer. "Past is passed." But they both knew that wasn't true. As much as she wanted to leave their decisions behind, there were two people whose lives were precariously balanced on the shifting pile of past sins.

Her phone indicated a text from Luca. *Got signal. Buckle up.*

They followed Luca toward the blazing horizon.

*Lord, please help us find them.*

*Fast.*

# SEVEN

Tate pressed down the black feelings in his gut. Anger at Bittman, shame at his own failure toward both Maria and Stephanie and an unaccountable sense of betrayal that Stephanie had delivered herself into Bittman's world. He knew it didn't make sense. He'd been so desperate to keep her from knowing the truth of his humiliating addiction that he'd practically shoved her away, buried in his own grief at the death of his father.

The sound of the most horrible moment of his life echoed in his ears. He'd driven to see her, mind fogged on painkillers. Even in that altered state, his heart craved her, the need overriding common sense. After an incoherent ramble about how sorry he was, she'd begged him not to drive, pulling at his arm, trying to snatch the keys. He had to get away, to keep from shaming himself any further.

He'd wrenched free, floored the gas pedal, and then somehow she'd been there, in front of him and he couldn't stop in time. He remembered the soft thump of her body hitting the front fender, the blood oozing from her cheek. He'd managed one word, one agonizing plea. *Help.* And then it had all gone mercifully black.

He swallowed the nausea that came with the memory. God saved her from him, he was sure. Was He systematically removing all the people in Tate's life? His father, Stephanie, his sister? Where was the compassionate, loving guardian his mother always told him about? Once you accepted Christ, as he'd done as a teen, wasn't He supposed to help you, no matter what? Bring people into your life to mentor and guide you? When the addiction took hold of him with stunning ferocity, it seemed to drive away everyone close to him.

Now he was alone, and that's the way it would stay.

The miles unrolled in front of them. Stephanie remained busy on her laptop, and he dutifully tailed Luca. It was more comfortable for them both to be immersed in their own worlds.

"Guarneri made several instruments before he died in 1741, but the one that may or may not have burned at Hans's shop, the Quinto Guarneri, was unique. It was almost lost in a building collapse in the early 1800s, but amazingly it survived with only a slight scar on the scroll." She checked her messages again. Only one from Brooke, which she listened to attentively. "Victor's coming around," she relayed, relief shining on her face until a shadow of disappointment followed. "He can't remember what happened." She bit her lip. "He keeps asking for Dad."

Tate put a hand on her arm. "We'll get him back. Both of them."

She didn't look at him, but clasped his hand with hers. For a moment, hands twined together, it felt like old times. He was her rock, the rebellious love that would give his life for hers in a heartbeat. Her stomach let out a loud rumble, and her cheeks pinked. "I never did get to eat any of that pie."

"Under your seat there's a box of food. Take what you want."

She raised an eyebrow. "You never used to plan ahead much for road trips."

"Still don't. It's Gilly's truck. He doesn't leave home without a week's supply. He got trapped in an elevator during the Loma Prieta quake, and he vowed never to be without food again."

She slid open the compartment under the seat and grabbed a couple granola bars and a box of Oreos. "I'm going to give Gilly a kiss when I see him," she said, taking a big bite of the granola bar.

Tate chuckled. "I'm sure that will make his decade. He's had the hots for my sister for years, and she's never given him a second look. Too bad. He's geeky, but he'd treat her much better than the other guys."

He avoided looking at her.

"Tate, I know Luca would never take advantage of a woman. He didn't touch Maria, and he certainly didn't try to force himself on her."

Tate's jaw clenched. "She says he did."

Stephanie tried to tread lightly. "She is…volatile. A week after she said that about Luca, she was involved with Bittman."

"I know she's made mistakes, but past is passed, just like you said. And we're supposed to be forgiven, right? That Christian thing?"

His tone was suddenly earnest, and something in his gray eyes was soft and tender. "Yes, that's right." She wondered again why it was harder to forgive someone you loved than a complete stranger. Her heart sped up a tic, and she realized she was actually pleased to have Tate sitting here next to her, clean of the painkillers that nearly destroyed him. Maybe he really had beaten his addiction. On impulse, she traced a finger across the toughened skin of his hand. He jerked, shooting her a look she could not decipher, but he didn't move his hand away.

He shifted on the seat. "There's water in my backpack."

She snagged it from the backseat and rummaged around

inside, rifling through a clean shirt and a small travel case. Her heart stopped when she saw the bottle in the bottom of the pack. She read the label. Painkillers. Hating herself for doing it, she gently poked at it. The tiny sound of the pills shifting inside mirrored the crash of her own emotions. Half full.

He was still using. Maybe not at that moment, or even that day, but he would soon enough. The thought burned inside her.

"Find some?"

She'd always considered herself courageous, but in that moment she found she could not bear to confront him. She forced a smile and pulled a water bottle from the pack. "Yes, thanks." There were no tears forming in her eyes, no rage at herself for believing he'd gone straight. Only sadness and despair. She prayed silently that God would take away his burden because she now realized he did not have the strength to do it himself, and he probably never would.

"Something wrong?" he asked.

"Nothing that won't be fixed when we find my father and Maria," she said, turning her eyes out the windshield, watching the evening swallow up the day.

Tate finally followed Luca into a dark parking lot, home to a truck stop diner and a gas pump. They stayed at the far end of the lot, hidden by a screen of semitrailers. He'd kept a close eye on the rearview mirror and had seen no one tailing them, though the fact that Bittman was somehow keeping tabs on Stephanie's every move made a knot in his stomach.

Luca joined them, staying away from the parking lot lights. "Ricardo's stopped here. I saw him look around, check his watch. He's meeting someone."

Tate's hopes lifted. "Maria?"

"Or maybe the crazy man from Devlin's music shop. I

think Ricardo paid Devlin a visit, and Devlin's afraid Bittman will find out and think he's double crossing."

"Let's go in and see for ourselves," Tate said, starting for the door.

"No, we wait here. We don't want to spook him."

Tate stiffened. "We've done enough waiting and following. We can't let him get away."

"He won't. His car is here. We wait." Luca's eyes glittered. "This is how we do things."

"You're a Treasure Seeker, Luca, not a private eye."

"It's oftentimes the same thing." Luca cocked his head. "We've found everything from paintings to a million-dollar stamp, so maybe you should step back and let us do our job."

They waited, the minutes ticking into hours until Tate was nearly ready to jump out of his skin. He was about to walk into the restaurant with or without Luca's consent, when Stephanie's phone rang. After a fleeting look of fear, she answered it. They watched as her eyes widened.

"But why don't you just tell me over the phone? What's the big discovery?" She listened, alternately cajoling and demanding. Finally she hung up. "The man mailed Devlin a picture of the violin. He's insisting we go see him in person."

"When?" Tate said.

"Now." She checked her watch. "It's an hour back to Lone Ridge, so we'll be there by ten if we leave right away."

"It could be a trap," Tate said.

"We don't have a choice," Stephanie shot back.

Luca's eyes danced in thought. "We'll have to split up."

"I'll go back with Steph. You stay on Ricardo," Tate said, retrieving his keys from a front pocket.

Luca hesitated, shooting a look at his sister.

She shrugged, and Tate felt a slice of pain at her obvious reluctance, but she acquiesced. "It makes sense since you've got the signal on him. If he does leave unexpectedly, you can track it."

"Be careful," Luca said to Stephanie.

*I won't let anything happen to her,* he wanted to say. It would have been false assurance. Besides, Luca would never trust him again after he'd almost killed Stephanie. Tate was not sure he fully trusted himself, for that matter.

*It's just a drive. Take her, get the info and bring her back.* He put a hand on the small of her back to guide her, wishing his fingers didn't relish the play of muscles there, wondering when the riveting movement of her dark hair would cease to mesmerize him.

Probably never, the same way he would never stop missing her, stop feeling the pain of his leg, which seemed somehow twined with the ache in his heart. The past is passed, but it was also unchangeable and unforgettable. He shut the door after her, which elicited an exasperated look from Stephanie, like it always had.

"I can shut my own door," she'd perpetually insisted.

"My mother taught me right," he'd responded a million times. A lady deserves that much, and she deserved so much more.

She was oddly quiet on the way back to Lone Ridge, tapping keys on her computer or gazing out the window onto the road, which was now only lit by a fat yellow moon.

A car zipped by going the other way as they approached the town, which was quiet and still.

"First car we've seen in miles," he said with a twinge of uneasiness.

"Mmm," she murmured.

He pulled the truck to a stop a couple blocks from the music store. "Best not to be too obvious."

"In case Bittman has someone watching, like he did at the restaurant? I don't trust him."

Tate drummed his fingers on the steering wheel.

Stephanie took a small pair of binoculars out of her pocket and trained them on the music store. "Looks dark."

"Could be we're early."

"It's ten-fifteen." She put a hand on the car's door release. "Let's check it out."

He stopped her. "Why don't we watch awhile first? Take our time."

Her mouth tightened into a luscious bow. "Because we don't have any time to spare. My father isn't eating, your sister is still missing and someone else is searching for the treasure that I'm going after."

She was out the door before he could say another word. He followed, trying to keep from stepping on the numerous small twigs that littered the walkway to the music store. The place was dark, windows shuttered.

He caught up with her as she knocked softly.

"Mr. Devlin?" she called. After a moment, she knocked louder and called again.

"Maybe he's gone home."

She shook her head, face pale in the moonlight. "He lives here, in a room in back."

He didn't ask how she knew, but he did manage to get ahead of her as she made her way toward the rear of the store. They saw it at the same time—the gleam of lamplight, showing from underneath a curtained window.

She tapped on the rear door and called Devlin's name again.

No answer. She dialed Devlin's number on her cell phone. They both heard it ringing inside, two rings, three, five before the answering machine came on. Stephanie pocketed the phone, her look mirroring the concern he felt.

"Something's not right," he whispered, mouth pressed to the delicate shell of her ear. "We should get back in the truck, wait and see what develops." He knew she wouldn't go for it, though.

Ignoring him, she tried the handle. It turned.

"Unlocked," she breathed.

"Breaking and entering," he retorted.

"Since when did you get all concerned with the rules? You're still the same guy who stole a pig from the high school ag department."

"The pig came willingly, and I borrowed, not stole."

Her grin sent his heart spiraling. He grabbed her hands and pulled her closer until her mouth was inches from his. Fighting a wild desire to kiss her, he shook his head. "Steph, this isn't a good idea."

She cocked her head but didn't pull away. "Devlin told us to come. He might be in there needing help."

"Or it might be someone else waiting. We don't know all the players involved."

She inched closer. "I'm going in there," she breathed, causing his body to tingle all over.

He held her tighter. "Let me. You stay outside with the phone. I'll yell if I need help."

She gave him an odd look. "I wish you would have told me you needed help before."

He felt confused. "I don't know what you mean."

"The pills," she said, eyes moist.

He stepped back. "I beat it by myself. I didn't need your help."

"And you don't need it now?" she whispered. She closed the gap and pressed her cheek to his. "Forget it. I'll go in and you stay in the truck."

He closed his eyes against the softness of her skin, the silken touch of her hair on his cheeks. Raindrops on roses. She was still the most beautiful thing he had ever seen, felt or come near to in his whole life. He pretended for a split second that she was his again, that his heart was whole and clean, cleaved once more with hers. When the feeling became too much to bear, he gently set her back.

*Stop deluding yourself, Tate. Those are just memories of old feelings. Things are different now.*

"Steph…"

It was a mistake. As soon as he released her, she turned the knob and darted into the silent building.

# EIGHT

Stephanie tried to get her bearings. It was not the dim interior that confused her senses, but the way her body reacted to Tate's touch. He was an addict, and she could not allow him in her life again. That was clear, but why did her body seem so reluctant to get the message? She took a deep breath and willed her pulse to simmer down.

Tate stepped in behind her and they both stood still, listening. The soft hum of voices startled her until she saw Tate mouth the word *radio*. They stood in a minuscule kitchen, the sink filled with water and submerged cookware. A rickety table and chair stood off in the corner, littered with an untidy pile of sheet music and a plate smeared with something that might have been dried ketchup.

The kitchen had two exits. One led out to the store area, and the other must lead to Devlin's private room, where the light gleamed from under the slightly open door. She made a move toward the bedroom, but in a flash Tate was in front of her, crouched low, pushing the door open.

He managed to keep her behind him until he'd poked in his head. Then she pushed past and into the room which housed a cot and small end table, yet another stack of sheet music, an odd collection of hardware from various instruments and a chipped coffee mug. On the wall was a calendar of famous golf courses of the world, the page set to three months prior. In the corner, an old golf club and a bucket of balls were propped.

Stephanie was at the desk, sorting through the odd scribbled papers and moving aside piles of bills. "Nothing here of substance," she whispered.

He picked up a mug. "Still warm."

Her eyes widened. With an unspoken agreement, they left the bedroom and made their way toward the store. Once again they paused to listen before they pushed aside the door. The air was stuffy, the smell of mildew strong. Tate turned on the flashlight and beamed it around, looking into the spaces large enough for an intruder to hide. Large shapes covered with sheets gleamed back at them. Instruments, she imagined, but looking more like pale beasts in the gloom.

Tate was sidling around to the counter in the back corner, where they had first met Devlin. It would make the perfect hiding spot for Devlin, or someone else. There was no moonlight to help now, since long floor-to-ceiling drapes covered the front windows.

She wanted to call out, to ease Devlin's mind if he was indeed cowering on the dingy tile floor behind the counter. But there were others in the game. Maria was after the prize, and Ricardo was a player who was as determined to find the violin as the Treasure Seekers, a man who might be willing to kill in order to obtain it.

Tate was inches from the counter now, and she tugged at his belt loop. He looked over, face swimming in shadows. She opened her mouth to whisper...what? To be careful? Tate wasn't careful and never had been. It was part of the reason she'd loved him.

*Past tense, Stephanie. He's history, and this is your investigation.* She quickly danced around him and approached the counter. Grabbing a handful of music from a shelf, she tossed the sheets on the countertop. There was no startled movement, no sudden fluttering of a stranger hiding there.

She stuck her head over the top, Tate right at her side.

No one was there.

Stephanie sighed as Tate turned on a nearby lamp. "He's gone, but recently."

She went to pull aside the curtain and get a look at the street. Something solid met her fingers—a figure behind the curtain. She let out a cry as the figure, head covered by a knit cap, shoved by her, knocking her to the ground, heading for the back of the shop.

Tate rushed after, knocking over a wastebasket, which slowed him down momentarily.

By the time Stephanie made it to her feet, they had both shot out the back door and into the night. She took off after them, disconcerted when she exploded into the darkened yard, startling an owl from its perch on the limb overhead.

The yard emptied into a wild space behind Devlin's store, flat ground peppered with desert holly and folding down into a dry ridge straddling a gorge. It didn't provide much cover, or much of an escape avenue. The front would make more sense. She jogged along the pebbled stepping stones to the street, which was eerily quiet. The truck was still there, so Tate had pursued on foot. Ears straining, she could not decide which direction they had gone.

Her heart hammered in her chest, body frozen with indecision. The only reasonable plan was to drive the streets until she found them, but she had no keys. Had Tate left them in the truck? She scurried around to the driver's side. Just as she grasped the handle, she felt someone behind her.

She whirled to find herself face-to-face with a young woman. The girl's long hair was spilling loose from the knit cap, her dark eyes wide and scared. She clutched at Stephanie's forearms.

"Go home. Both of you. Go home and it will be okay, I promise."

Stephanie fought through her surprise. "Tell me what's going on."

She shook her head and looked around. "I can't explain it right now. Just get out of here before you get hurt. Tell Tate."

"No, you're going to tell him." Stephanie grabbed the girl's wrist. "If you're running from Bittman, it's a matter of time before he finds you." She tried to pull her toward the store but the girl resisted, yanking so ferociously that Stephanie lost her grip and took a step backward.

The younger girl stood for a moment in the street, eyes gleaming in the moonlight. "I know what I'm doing. You're putting us all in danger by being here. Go home," she hissed once more before she whirled and ran away into the darkness.

Tate sprinted into view, breathing hard. "Did you see which way he went?"

Stephanie swallowed. "Not he."

"What?"

"It wasn't Ricardo hiding behind the curtains, Tate. It was Maria."

They returned to the shop, Stephanie trailing Tate inside. She did not want to tell him his sister's message. It would only worsen his pain, but there was no way around it. He had to know. She related the conversation as best she could while he stood, arms crossed, taking it in. When she finished, he turned away, silent.

She went to him and put a hand on his shoulder, feeling the tension that turned his back muscles to steel. "We know she's safe for the moment. That's something."

He turned. "Safe? She's come here to steal from Bittman. How is that safe?"

Stephanie tried for a calming tone. "I know you were hoping it wasn't true."

He rubbed his hand across his face. "Yeah, I was hoping she was back home somewhere and Bittman was mistaken. Should have known."

She hated to see his helplessness. "We have to move forward, Tate, figure out what's going on and sort through it all. I'll call Luca and fill him in. See if there's been any movement from Ricardo."

He didn't answer. Instead he began to pace in restless circles around the periphery of the shop while she related the situation to her brother and learned that Ricardo was still inside the restaurant, though he had emerged several times to smoke a cigarette and make phone calls.

"So what happened to Devlin?" Luca demanded.

"That's the question of the day. He left here quickly." She lowered her voice. "Or someone took him."

Luca blew out a breath. "Maria must know."

"No doubt, but for the moment we don't know where she is, either. We'll drive through town, check around and then meet you." She disconnected and eyed Tate, who was now standing, arms folded, staring at the wall until he suddenly pulled out his phone and checked his messages.

"Text from Gilly. He says Maria hasn't touched her credit cards." Tate slammed the phone down on the counter and glowered. "Maybe Bittman is threatening Maria. She's trying to protect herself by running, not stealing his violin."

"Only one problem with that theory, Tate. Maria is here in Lone Ridge now, so she's involved all right—up to her neck."

His mouth tightened. "It's not what it looks like."

"Maybe it's not what you want to see. Denial is easy…" She broke off.

He blinked. "For an addict?" His words were soft, but they convicted her anyway. "I've done my share of denying, but this is my sister and I'm going to believe the best of her anyway, just like you'd do for your brothers."

She nodded. "I just hope you're not disappointed in the end."

"You need hope to be disappointed, and I lost that when I lost you."

The emotion came so quickly, she could not defend her heart against it. "I…"

"No guilt. My decisions, my choices. Right now, I've just got to look out for my sister." He moved away, scanning the walls of the shop, though she suspected his mind was far away.

*I lost that when I lost you.* She could not think of anything to say, staring at the tortured person before her, the remnants of the man who had been the anchor to her soul. *That was your mistake, Steph.*

Only God could be that anchor. No one was strong enough, not Luca, not Victor and not Tate Fuego, as much as she wanted him to be. She'd expected too much from him, invested too much in him and he'd let her down. Lesson learned.

She tore away her gaze. "I'll look in the back. Maybe Devlin left a note somewhere about where he was going." Without waiting for him, she marched into the kitchen, stomach still twisted in tight knots.

Devlin had been there recently, but so had Maria. If there was anything to find, she may already have snatched it. Recalling the dark look on Tate's face, she didn't think it would do any good to suggest it. She rifled the piles of papers again and sorted through Devlin's files, feeling more like a nosy relative than an investigator. A half hour later she was ready to pull the plug. It was nearly two o'clock in the morning, and the day was catching up with her. Fatigue and the tension between them seemed to weigh down her limbs. Her stomach felt alternately hungry and sick with fear. Time ticked away relentlessly. She mumbled a prayer for her father, for Victor... She cast a glance to the darkened store area and added a prayer for Tate and his sister.

Would Maria's bad decisions be too much for him to bear? Would it end this time in a tragic overdose? With fingers gone cold, she returned the pile of papers she'd been sifting through to their place and went back to the shop.

"Can't find anything," she said. "Let's go before someone calls the cops on us."

He nodded and moved with her, but stopped abruptly, staring at the wall.

"What is it?"

He pointed to the yellowed picture of Devlin's old shop, the one he'd noticed before that tied Devlin to Bittman's father, Hans. For a moment, she thought he was going to remove the picture and take it with them, but his fingers plucked something from behind—a stiff square slid behind the photo with only a small edge showing.

She crowded next to him as they shone a flashlight on the square. It was a Polaroid snapshot of a violin. Stephanie's breath hitched up a notch. "This must be what he called us about. Something in this picture was a revelation to him."

Tate pocketed the photo. "You were right before. We need to go now. We'll take a closer look, but not here."

She followed him out and they closed the door, making their way to the truck. Stephanie used her penlight to scrutinize the photo as they drove, but the light was poor. The silence between them lasted the whole hour's return trip until they met Luca, who was leaning against the side of the rental car. Stephanie recognized the tension in her brother, tension that often arose after long periods of inactivity.

He straightened as they emerged, and Stephanie showed him the photo. "It's got to be the Guarneri."

"As near as I can tell. It's not a great picture and I'll need better light to examine it, but that's my guess. It's our first solid proof that we're on the right track."

"No more calls from Devlin? Maybe he got spooked when Maria showed up, stashed the photo and ran."

Tate shook his head. "My sister didn't threaten him. I think she was there looking, too."

"Maybe," Luca said slowly.

A dusty semi rolled onto the property, momentarily drowning out their conversation. They waited until it parked, the driver and passenger lost in shadow as they headed toward the restaurant.

"Ricardo seems to be getting more agitated. He comes out every ten minutes or so to look around. Whoever is meeting him is late." They continued to watch for another fifteen minutes until a banged-up Volkswagen Bug rumbled from the back parking lot and vanished into the darkness. "I'm going to take a look inside," Luca said. "I've got a bad feeling. Watch Ricardo's car."

Stephanie did not want to endure any more painful exchanges with Tate, but she knew making an obvious entrance might cause Ricardo to bolt.

A man with a thick black beard came out of the restaurant as Luca went in. Stephanie pretended to talk on her phone as the man approached Ricardo's sedan.

He casually pulled out a set of keys, took a look around and let himself in. Tate caught him by the sleeve and yanked him out before he could turn the key.

"Whatsa matter with you?" the man spluttered, his arm raised in a fist. "I got nothing worth stealing, man. You got the wrong sucker."

Stephanie held up a calming hand. "We're not going to rob you. This car doesn't belong to you. How did you get the keys?"

A sly smile appeared under the tangle of beard.

"Did you steal them?" Tate demanded.

"Nuh-uh. He gave 'em to me."

Tate pressed closer. "Who?"

"Guy in the diner. Traded me."

Stephanie's heart sank. "Traded you for what?"

The man laughed. "My old clunker. Told me I could have his wheels if I'd give him mine. Nice trade, huh?"

Stephanie groaned. "What type of car did you have?"

The grin appeared again. "My old VW Bug. Sweet, huh?"

Tate exchanged a look with Stephanie.

They'd been beaten. Again.

# NINE

Tate exchanged an exasperated look with Stephanie. It could not be that Ricardo had evaded them again. There was another piece of information that he was reluctant to ask for, but had no choice. "Was the guy who traded cars with you alone?"

"Yep."

Tate let out a relieved sigh.

Scratching his head, the man continued. "Until some long-haired chick came in. Their talk was real serious like, and that's when he came over to my table, paid for my dinner and traded cars. Left right after. I finished my ice cream and came out to enjoy my new wheels." His eyes narrowed. "Got a problem with that?"

Stephanie shook her head. "No, no problem. Is it okay if I look in the car for a minute? Just to see if the man left anything in there? He's an…acquaintance of ours."

He shrugged. "Go ahead, but if he left any cash, it's mine fair and square. A trade's a trade."

Tate rolled around the facts in his mind while Stephanie searched the car. Maria left Devlin's shop and thumbed a ride with the semi driver. She scooted into the restaurant, right under their noses, and convinced Ricardo to ditch his car. His sister was smart, too smart for her own good—but not smart enough to keep herself from partnering with Ricardo. He felt like slamming a fist on the car hood.

Luca jogged out. "Hostess told me Ricardo and Maria left by the back exit."

"In a VW Bug they bartered for," Stephanie said miserably as she got out of Ricardo's car with a creased road map in her hand.

Tate's self-control snapped. "So I guess your tracking device isn't worth two cents now. Treasure Seekers isn't worth much, either." Frustration rose in him like the clouds of dust kicked up by the VW as it drove away. "Computers, fancy cars, the people you're paying. It turns out to be nothing but show." He'd expected outrage, anger—hoped for it really, a way to release the emotions building inside, a wall for him to slam into.

Luca looked more surprised than angry. "So that's what your problem is? Money? You resent the fact that we've got resources?"

"No," he said, looking away.

Luca must have read some truth in his voice. "I think that's it. You got a chip on your shoulder because of our net worth. It's always goaded you, hasn't it, Tate?"

Tate's teeth clenched. "You're no better than me."

Luca raised an eyebrow. "I know that and you never heard me say it, did you? Or imply anything of the kind? Ask Stephanie, and she'll tell you the same thing. The problems we have with you, Tate, have nothing to do with your finances. Whatever inferiority complex you've got going is of your own making, so don't lay it at my doorstep."

Tate walked away a few paces, sucking in air, rage giving over to some other emotion. Much as he wanted to, he could not fault Luca, true enough. The decision four years ago, the last-minute switch of vehicles with his father, could not be foisted off on Luca as much as he desperately wanted it to be. The naked truth was, Tate had convinced his father to let him use the car because he was embarrassed to take Stephanie to a Gage family picnic in his own battered Ford pickup.

It was a decision driven by the same shame that made him avoid their other family invitations, excuse himself from certain Gage events. He was not of their strata. He'd thought he'd read it in their eyes, but maybe he was seeing only his own feelings reflected there. He rubbed his callused hands against his jeans, his father's words coming back to him.

*"The greatest man was a carpenter."*

Tate remembered the way his father's hands looked, scarred and leathery, strong. *"You're worthy because He said so."*

Worthy. He tried on the idea as if it was a new jacket laid across his shoulders, and for a split second, he felt straighter, stronger. Worthy of respect? From Stephanie? From the Gage family? From the sister he'd failed? Flickers of the past shot through his mind, the pills he'd swallowed, the sight of Stephanie lying on the pavement, the accident that killed his father. Bottom line was, he'd convinced his father to drive the pickup, and that same pickup experienced brake failure on a steep section of sandy road. His father was dead. The hunger for comfort ate at him—a need which had previously sent him to the medicine cabinet.

*You don't use pills anymore. You're going to fight through it, every day, every minute, like you have for the past year.*

Looking over at Luca and Stephanie, he wished he could tell them.

*I'm clean, and I'm going to stay that way.*

Their heads were bent together, a team, a family.

"You had your chance, Tate," he whispered to himself.

Stephanie gestured for him to follow, and they headed into the diner.

"Going to ask some more questions?"

"No, going to get something to eat before I keel over," she said. "We know where they're headed anyway."

He nodded. "Bitter Song."

"Right. So I may as well not drop dead of starvation on the way." She took the lead, and he smothered a smile. He'd learned way back in high school that Stephanie, petite as she was, did not do well skipping meals. His own stomach growled, and he kept up the pace.

The waiter at the counter was a skinny teen with hair to his shoulders. He took their order of sandwiches for Luca and Stephanie and a burger for Tate, to go. When he sauntered off, Stephanie pulled out the Polaroid and squinted at it.

"Not a good quality photo." She flipped it over. "No notes or dates on the back."

"Just looks like a violin to me," Tate said.

She held the photo closely. "I can see a gleam of white here, a scrap lying next to the instrument." She held it so they could see. Her eyes shone. "Could be a label."

"Proving what?" Luca asked, taking a sip of tea.

"The Guarneri family labeled most of their instruments. Generally it was a piece of handmade paper, and the text was in Latin. It would authenticate this treasure we've been killing ourselves to find."

Tate raised an eyebrow. "If this thing is from the 1700s, would the label have survived?"

"It's possible." Stephanie considered it. "The labels were attached inside the instruments. Do you have a magnifying glass, Luca?"

He shook his head. "Didn't think to bring one. Maybe we can get hold of one in Bitter Song."

She started pacing. "I wish they'd hurry up with that order. I need to get my hands on a magnifying glass."

"It's going on three in the morning. Where do you expect to find an open store in Bitter Song at this hour?"

She flashed him a smile that made his stomach tighten. "I'm a very resourceful gal. Ask anyone."

He didn't need to ask. She was resourceful and beautiful, and he was not surprised that her beauty had not waned one iota in the years they'd been apart. Now it seemed he would be shoulder to shoulder with Stephanie in the next leg of their adventure.

He had a feeling that finding an eighteen-million-dollar violin in the middle of the desert might just be the easy part of the trip.

Stephanie's phone buzzed and she clicked it on, unable to resist a smile as the gruff voice rumbled through the cell.

"I hate the desert. Too many bugs," Tuney said.

"You hate everything. It's good to talk to you."

He grunted, voice softening. "How you holding up, kiddo?"

"Okay, but we need this to be over. Do you have anything for us?"

She heard a crunching noise, and she knew the crotchety private eye was munching on his favorite snack, animal crackers.

"Matter of fact, I do."

Stephanie straightened, and both Luca and Tate caught her excitement.

"Had a talk with one Roger Goldberg, who is an incredibly annoying mechanic who happens to be a friend of a certain helicopter pilot who works for this Bittman character."

Her eyes widened. "What did he say?"

"Seems his buddy mentioned he had a flight to do in San Francisco for the boss on that Wednesday afternoon."

"Did Roger know the end destination?"

"No, Bittman scares his people enough that they know not to blab too many details."

Her stomach dropped. "Oh."

"But he does happen to know it was someplace local because he met the guy for an early dinner that same day."

She gripped the phone. "So Bittman didn't have my father taken out of the area. He's being held nearby. Maybe even in San Francisco."

"Looks that way, doesn't it?"

"Tuney, you're wonderful." She relayed the information to the others. "How did you ever get Roger to tell you all that?"

Tuney laughed. "Trade secrets, but tell your brother he's going to loan me that fancy fishing boat of his for a good long while."

"I'll tell him."

Tuney's voice sobered. "This isn't done. San Francisco is forty-six square miles, and I'm going to cover every last one until I find your father."

Stephanie's throat thickened. "Thank you." Luca was gesturing for the phone, and she knew he would call in more people to help with the search. "Just remember, Bittman is…"

"I know—ruthless as a starving piranha. Well, guess what? I'm pretty ruthless myself, not to mention ornery, and no one scares me off a case."

She thanked him again and handed the phone to Luca, blinking back tears.

Tate took her hand and squeezed. "Staying strong?"

She felt the aching comfort of his touch ripple through her body before she withdrew her hand, nodding vigorously. "Absolutely," she said, ignoring the twisting in her stomach. She knew he was watching her, and she could not stand the feeling of those intense gray eyes on her for one more moment.

Leaving Luca to make arrangements with Tuney, Stephanie excused herself to visit the restroom. She saw her own reflection in the mirror, and for a moment did not recognize herself. Her hair was wild, eyes shadowed with fatigue, face drawn with worry. Every hour that passed brought them closer to the violin, but it meant another hour that her father was under the power of the crazy Joshua Bittman.

She splashed water on her face and tried to fix a positive thought in her mind. He was probably fine; his stubborn, irascible personality had seen him through many a rocky time in his life, including the death of their mother when Stephanie was a baby.

A lady with ash blond hair entered and smiled as she washed her hands.

Stephanie smiled back, but did not encourage any conversation. She wanted to get on the road without any further delay.

"Visiting?"

Stephanie started. "What?"

"You're not from around here." The woman's eyes played over Stephanie's jeans and jacket. "On vacation?"

"Business trip."

The woman smiled, and there was something sly in the expression. Stephanie's skin prickled.

"Most people don't come to the desert for business," the lady said, painting a coat of pink onto her lips.

Stephanie quickly dried her hands.

The woman stepped between Stephanie and the door. "But then, you don't look like most people. Where are you headed?"

Pulse thudding, Stephanie took in her size—she wasn't big, but she looked strong. Her hand was in the pocket of her jacket. "Not sure."

The woman moved closer—close enough that Stephanie could smell her perfume, a heavy floral. "I thought you were a business woman, but you don't know where you're going?" She inched one more step, crowding Stephanie back toward the stalls.

Stephanie forced a smile. "Sorry, in a hurry."

"That's not very friendly." Keeping one hand in her pocket, she brought the other to her face, long nails tapping thoughtfully on her front teeth. "What kind of business are you in anyway?"

"The kind that's not your business," Stephanie said.

The woman put her hand in her purse and pulled out a knife. "Suppose I make it my business."

Stephanie eased back as much as she could and got into a ready position. She'd practiced the scenario many times in her mixed martial arts class.

The woman's eyes flickered as she caught the movement. "You some kind of Bruce Lee?"

"No," Stephanie said. "But I'm good enough to get that knife out of your hand and take you down in the process."

The would-be assailant hesitated before she slipped the knife back in her purse. "I'm not getting paid enough for that."

Stephanie kept her ready stance. "Who paid you and why?"

"Dunno his name," she said with a shrug. "Just told me to slow you up. I wasn't really going to hurt you."

"Silver crew cut?"

"Yeah. Gal's gotta make a living somehow. No hard feelings?"

Stephanie didn't bother to answer. With a quick movement, she elbowed the woman aside and escaped into the hallway. She made her way quickly back and found her brother and Tate waiting. The lady did not emerge from the restroom.

"Let's go, right now," she said, nearly sprinting for the door.

"What's going on?" Tate asked, falling in behind her.

"Some lady in the bathroom was paid by Ricardo to give me a hard time."

Luca took her shoulder and turned her around. "Did she hurt you?"

"No, but she thought about it for a while." Stephanie felt another rush of prickles along her arms. "Bittman has people everywhere, keeping tabs on us, and now Ricardo is getting in on that game."

Though Luca and Tate both wanted to look for the woman, Stephanie convinced them not to. "We've got to get to Bitter Song. Maria and Ricardo are already there, and I want to get a feel for things before we decide on a plan for tomorrow—actually today."

She glanced over her shoulder, but there was still no sign of the woman. "Besides, the longer we stay here, the more information is reported back to Bittman or Ricardo."

Resisting the urge to run, Stephanie exited the restaurant, back out into the cool air. The sky was a brilliant, star-spangled velvet over their heads, and she breathed deep. Tate was at her elbow. Though he didn't touch her, she felt his presence strongly, like the cool breeze on her face.

When Luca steered her toward the rental car, she did not resist.

*Keep as much distance between you and Tate as you can.*

It was a relief to slide into the darkened car interior. Luca started the engine, and she leaned back her head, suddenly overwhelmed by fatigue. Then an email popped up on her phone. Just a photo, no message.

Cold fear squeezed the breath from her. It was a picture of a handkerchief. She held the phone up to Luca with trembling fingers. "It's Daddy's," she whispered. "I gave it to him on his last birthday."

The dark corner of the photo showed black, illuminated by the dome light Luca flipped on.

They looked at each other in horror, transfixed by the spot that looked very much like blood, an ugly blot against the sheen of the silk.

# TEN

Bitter Song lived up to its name, as far as Tate could see when he awoke just before dawn the next morning, stiff from sleeping in the tiny area in the back of the truck covered by a camper shell. The temperature was chilly in spite of their desert location. He hadn't wanted to admit that he didn't have the money to rent one of the small rooms at the Desert Spur Inn, where they'd arrived only a couple hours before. He knew if he'd said something, Luca and Stephanie would have paid for his room without any comment. Probably stupid to refuse, but he had to hang on to his remaining self-respect with every ounce of strength he possessed.

He turned his back on these thoughts and sucked in a deep lungful of clean desert air. All he really needed anyway was a bed and access to the small shower in the pool area. A dark-haired and sun-weathered guy had been cleaning the pool deck with slow, deliberate strokes when Tate had helped himself to the shower earlier. He hadn't said anything.

The stinging hot water hadn't washed away the image. He'd gotten the gist of the final shock, the delivery of the handkerchief photo. Bittman was playing a sick game, and it made his blood boil. The thought that Maria was involved in the mess added salt to the wound. There was still no further word from Gilly, and Tate had tried again several times to leave messages for Maria, just in case she was checking. He'd wanted to say something along the lines of, "What's the matter with you? Don't you know who you're tangled up with? Ricardo's no better than Bittman."

His own words surprised him.

*Sis, I know I've been harsh on you. I'm sorry. Let me help you. Call me, please.*

He gazed out into the stark landscape of sand flats, distant canyons and the abrupt range of mountains that punched into the rapidly lightening sky. The inn seemed to be perched on the edge of a vast nowhere, bisected by a ribbon of road that led to the half-dozen buildings that comprised downtown. It was almost as if the great Mojave Desert was in the process of swallowing up the town like a snake ingesting a helpless rodent—like Bittman would do to his sister if he didn't find a way to put a stop to it.

He shook his head and did a few stretches to try to work out the stiffness in his leg, wondering why he didn't see any sign of life from the two rooms occupied by Luca and Stephanie. They were exhausted, pushed to the limit by fear and fatigue, but he did not think it was enough to keep Stephanie in bed.

He was proven right when he finally noticed them sitting under the shade offered by a sun-bleached umbrella stuck in a ragged patch of grass, a makeshift picnic area for weary travelers, perched on the far edge of the parking lot. She saw him and gestured him over.

Luca's attention was fixed on his laptop screen, but Stephanie had a curved piece of glass in her hands, and she peered through it to the picture below—the picture Devlin had left in the shop.

"You found yourself a magnifying glass?"

She shook her head, nose wrinkled as she squinted. "I

took the makeup mirror apart in the bathroom and borrowed the glass."

"I always said if life didn't give you a door, you'd make a window." He laughed. "Why didn't I think of that?"

"Probably because you don't have any use for makeup mirrors. Can you read this?" She took his hand and pulled him down on the bench next to her, where he tried hard not to feel the softness of her body pressed next to his as he stared through the glass.

"Just looks like squiggles to me." She pressed her face to his, and the sensation made his stomach tumble.

"There," she breathed. "Doesn't that look like letters?"

The satin of her skin next to his made him want to hold her face with his hands and press her lips to his. "Too small to read," he muttered as he stood, pacing up and down the small area.

Stephanie continued to stare at the scrap of paper.

Tate circled until he could stand it no longer. "Time's a wasting. We're going after the crazy desert guy today, right? Shouldn't we get started?"

Luca looked up from his screen. "That's what I'm doing. Checking law enforcement records and newspaper references for anything having to do with a Guarneri."

Tate shook his head. "How about we just go look for some crazy guy with a violin? How many could there be in the desert?"

Luca sighed. "Treasure hunting is mostly research—weeding through historical documents, diaries, talking to someone's great grandfather. You've got to be methodical."

"We're looking for a fiddle, not the lost treasure of the Aztecs."

"An eighteen-million-dollar fiddle, and this is not something we're going to find with 3-D deep-seeking metal detectors and radar units. We have to do some groundwork, otherwise we're just wasting time. We've got to think smart here." He turned back to the laptop.

Tate burned with restlessness. He wasn't about to sit still staring at pieces of paper and computer screens when his sister was running around the desert, working with a possible murderer.

He let himself into the pool area. "Hey," he said, giving a friendly nod to the worker.

The man nodded and offered a polite smile.

"We're looking for someone who lives around here. A guy with a beard. Know anyone like that?"

The man shook his head. "No."

"You sure?"

He nodded again and moved to the trash can, pulling out the filled bag and inserting a new one. Tate moved closer.

"Look, I'm going to level with you. My sister's in a lot of trouble, and this guy can help me figure out where she is. I don't want to make trouble for him—all I want to do is help my sister."

The man looked up, a web of wrinkles appearing around his narrowed eyes as he took in Tate's full measure, from his worn boots to his faded baseball cap. "You got a limp, I seen you. What happened?"

"Tried to get my dad out of a car wreck. The explosion shattered my femur. My sister is all I've got left."

He considered. "She got hurt in the accident, too?"

Tate sighed. "Not on the outside."

"Sometimes the inside is worse." He picked up his broom and leaned against it. "I got a sister."

The man chewed his lip for a moment and crooked his finger in Tate's direction.

A squad car pulled up, and Stephanie had to blink several times to clear her vision from staring into the glass. "Luca…"

she breathed. There was no time to do anything but close the laptop and try to paste amiable looks on their faces before the cop got out, strolling by their cars before joining them at the table, her khaki uniform perfectly matching the shade of the gravel under her booted feet. An alert German shepherd looked out the open car window, eyes trained on his master, flared nostrils catching the airborne scents.

The officer stood, fingers tucked into her belt as sunlight found the crow's feet circling her eyes. She chewed a piece of white gum with quick movements of her jaw. "Good morning, I'm Officer Sartori. Welcome to Bitter Song."

Stephanie forced out the words. "Thank you. How nice to receive an official welcome."

"We aim to please. Enjoying your stay? Strange place for city folks to come and vacation."

"We like the desert," Luca said.

"Uh-huh." The officer shot them a smile that was completely devoid of humor. "I've got a substantial to-do list, so let's get down to it," she said, gesturing to the dog. "Bear doesn't like to be in the car very long."

Bear stiffened at the mention of his name.

Luca raised an eyebrow. "Is he liable to jump out of there when he gets bored?"

"Not from boredom, but if I start to sound stressed he's going to think about it, so why don't you give me the truth right off the proverbial bat? Why are you in Bitter Song, really?"

Luca waved his hand and offered a dazzling smile that would have caused many other women to melt. "Who wouldn't want to come here?"

Sartori's expression didn't change. She remained silent except for the cracking of her gum.

Stephanie exchanged a look with him. They could not lie to the police, but they might be able to avoid certain details.

"We own a Treasure Seekers business, and we followed an evidence trail to Bitter Song."

She pursed her lips. "Let me guess—you're looking for a violin, right?"

"How did you know that?" Stephanie said.

"Got a call from the sheriff at Lone Ridge this morning. He mentioned there had been a few visitors in town. We don't get many visitors." She continued chewing her gum, eyes scanning the table. "Love your bag. Coach?"

Stephanie swallowed hard. "Yes."

"Pretty. You visited the music store in Lone Ridge."

"We talked to Mr. Devlin and asked him if he had seen the violin."

"Had he?"

Sweat rolled down Stephanie's face. What if Bittman's contacts were watching right now? Reporting her conversation with the police?

"No," Luca cut in. "He'd spoken to someone who brought in a picture of a violin, but the man didn't leave an address and there was no way to verify the authenticity by a picture. We came to Bitter Song to ask around, see if we could dig up the name of the man Devlin talked to."

"Why did you go back to the music store last night? A resident saw your car there some time after midnight."

How much did Sartori know? Ice cold shivers went up Stephanie's back. "We got a phone message from him, and we went to meet him but he wasn't there."

Tate joined them and introduced himself. "Nice dog."

"Not nice. Effective," Sartori said. "I've seen him bring down a two-hundred-twenty-pound biker. Scared the guy so bad he wet his pants. You're Tate Fuego, the same Tate Fuego arrested for driving while under the influence of drugs four years ago?"

Stephanie watched the color suffuse Tate's face, and she

felt herself aching for him as their prior conversation replayed itself in her mind.

*Supposed to be forgiven, right? That Christian thing?*

If God forgave, why did his past sins keep getting dredged up for the all the world to see?

*Not past, Steph,* she told herself, remembering the pill bottle in his backpack.

"Yes, Officer," Tate was saying, chin high. "But I'm clean now. Have been for a year."

"Good. Hate to see a guy with plenty of miles ahead of him wipe out in the first leg of the race. Why are you with these two?"

Tate shrugged. "My sister is involved in looking for the violin, too. I want to be sure she stays out of trouble."

"It might just turn out that trouble's already here," Sartori said, the gum flashing between her teeth.

Stephanie felt a ripple of dread course through her. "What do you mean?"

"Early this morning the local cops recovered a body, victim of a hit-and-run. Two problems with that. First off, not too many hit-and-runs here. We're not exactly a speedway, you see."

"And the second problem?" Luca asked.

"Dead guy looked as though he'd been beaten before he was run down, like somebody was trying to get some information from him. Maybe he made a break from his attacker and met the front end of a vehicle."

Stephanie's stomach churned with dread as Sartori continued.

"Oh, and one other strange thing. Dead guy had your business card in his pocket." She pulled out a notebook and consulted it. "Treasure Seekers, proprietors Stephanie, Luca and Victor Gage." She stopped and quirked an eyebrow. "Where is Victor, anyway? You didn't bring along the other brother on this treasure hunt?"

Luca shook his head, eyes intense. "He's in the hospital recovering from an accident."

"And you're here in the Mojave? Chasing a violin? Strange priorities, if you don't mind me saying it."

Stephanie finally found her voice. "The dead man...who is he?"

Sartori cocked her head and gave her gum another good crack. "You know him. Bruno Devlin, owner of the music store you visited just last night."

Stephanie's cry hung for a moment in the thin desert air.

Sartori's expression remained relaxed, but Tate could see that her eyes didn't miss one single iota of their reactions.

"The poor man," Stephanie whispered.

"Yeah. Lived in Lone Ridge for years. Never caused a lick of trouble. Never even got so much as a parking ticket." Sartori stared at Stephanie.

"Did anyone see the car that hit him?" Luca asked.

"No, but you can believe I checked both your vehicles before I stopped to talk to you. So you have no idea why Mr. Devlin wanted to meet with you a second time?"

The moments ticked by. Tate waited to see if Stephanie would tell the rest about finding his sister in the shop and about finding the Polaroid, which she had hastily placed under a loose sheet of paper. She opened her mouth, and the agony unfolded on her face. The crackle of a radio on Sartori's belt broke the silence. She took a step away and listened before returning with a look of disgust on her face.

"Seems I've got to go. Somebody much higher on the food chain is rearranging my day." She leveled a deadly serious look at them. "Stay in touch. I'll be wanting to finish this conversation real soon." She got back into her cruiser and peeled out of the parking lot, bits of gravel zinging against the bottom of the car.

Luca waited until she was gone. "Who do you think is responsible for Devlin's death?"

"My money is on Ricardo," Tate said, eyes on Stephanie.

"But why kill him?" she mumbled. "He was just a man who sold instruments. He didn't have the violin."

"Maybe he knew where it was, and he was going to tell us."

Tate waited for the two of them to say it aloud, that Maria could have been the driver that struck and killed Devlin. The unspoken accusation hovered there until Luca got up from the bench and gave his sister a hug.

"I'm going to have Tuney make an anonymous call to the police and describe Ricardo and the VW. Maybe it will give them enough to work with. We've got to move faster, find the violin before someone else gets hurt or we're thrown in jail for obstruction."

"So let's go then," Tate said, pulling the keys from his pocket.

"Where?" Stephanie asked. "We have no leads."

"Speak for yourself. While you were sitting around, I did some research of my own."

Luca's eyes narrowed. "Really."

"Yes, really. Rocky, the janitor at this place, has worked here for fifteen years, and he knows everybody."

Stephanie's lips parted. "Everybody?"

"Yeah, including a man who goes by the name Eugene. Big guy, wiry beard, loves to hike up to the ruins and paint pictures. Even has a little place way outside of town."

Luca shook his head, but Tate thought he caught the slightest hint of admiration. "Good work, Fuego."

Tate couldn't resist. "Real good. I guess you'll have to put me on the Treasure Seekers' payroll pretty soon."

"Don't bet on it," Luca said, as he packed up his gear.

# ELEVEN

Stephanie had no luck finding the location Tate had been given for Eugene's home on her GPS. As near as they could glean from the elderly gas station attendant, there was a small stone structure about fifteen miles out of town that had been vacant for periods of time, but for the past few years was inhabited by a man matching Eugene's description.

"Have you spoken to him before?" Stephanie asked, pushing her wind-whipped bangs out of her face.

The attendant shrugged, arching a grizzled eyebrow. "Not much of a talker, except to himself. Carries around a sketch pad and scribbles all the time. Don't like people much. That's about all I know."

Stephanie thanked him and turned to go.

"Plays real nice, though," the attendant added.

Luca's eyebrows shot up. "Plays?"

The man nodded. "Yeah. I heard him one time when I was taking my grandkids out for a dune buggy ride around the stone house. We were resting in the shade near his place. Heard some sort of fiddle or something. Sounded real nice, but he stopped quick like when he heard us, I guess. As I said, he don't like people much."

"Thank you," she said. "You've been very helpful."

"One more word," he said, stabbing a callused thumb at the sky. "Better not go out there today."

"Why not?" Tate asked.

"Windy. Real windy. Not a good time to be out there near the dunes."

Stephanie nodded, and they returned to their cars. "Well, we're not calling off the search on account of a little wind."

Tate frowned, looking at the trees, their needles undulating like bristly fingers. "Sandstorms can kill you."

Luca shifted. "I don't know anything about them. I'm not a desert guy."

"Maria and I used to go with Dad and do some four-wheeling."

Stephanie saw the flash of pain ripple across his face and felt the urge to reach out to him, but she knew the gesture wouldn't be welcome.

He cleared his throat. "Anyway, we don't have a choice, do we? Clock's ticking down for your father and my sister."

Stephanie's stomach clenched. "And it's a matter of time before Sartori comes back with another set of questions we don't want to answer."

Silently they loaded up, she and Luca in the rental and Tate following in the truck. Luca headed in the direction the attendant had given them, down a dirt road that rose steadily in elevation against a brilliant sky, dotted with gossamer clouds. It was an arid, hostile environment, like an alien planet resistant to human life.

She closed her eyes for a moment, exhausted in body and spirit. *Daddy, where are you?* She prayed for the hundredth time that he was safe, that Victor would recover. That she could snatch her life back from Bittman's grasp. With her big brother beside her and Tate following behind, had she sucked them all into a goose chase that might come to a disastrous end?

When the panic began to threaten, she said another quick prayer and tried again to examine the photo Devlin had given her, but the bouncing of the car made it hard to focus.

"Who could have killed Devlin?" she mused aloud. "He was just a music store owner, not a threat to anyone."

"Ricardo might have killed him to keep him quiet, I suppose." Luca paused, then shot her a look. "There's another possibility, too."

Stephanie shook her head. "Maria is not a killer. She's impulsive and hot tempered, but she wouldn't do that."

Luca didn't look convinced. "When I politely declined a date, she told Tate that I came onto her. That doesn't say much for her character."

"She's desperate to have someone love her, Luca, and rejection freaks her out. I think that's why she fell in with Bittman. He was probably charming, gave her presents, a job, anything she wanted to string her along until he grew bored of her."

"So if she was in love with the guy, why go after his violin? What changed?"

Stephanie shaded her eyes against the sun-washed rock that rose on either side of the path. "That's what we'd better find out fast."

They drove for miles, climbing to the top of breathtaking vistas and back down to the endless acres of sand dunes, pushed along by the wind. Stephanie was beginning to worry that they'd made a wrong turn when they spotted a flat-topped stone structure, tucked into a dusty hollow below the road. Stephanie's heart sped up as she got out and they joined Tate, who was peering through a pair of binoculars.

"Doesn't look like anyone is home," he said, handing them to her.

She took a close look at the house, perched in the shade of a scraggly mesquite. There were only a few scrubby junipers growing close by, nothing to provide good cover. Wind tossed grit into her face, and she lowered the binoculars. "Any ideas?"

"Only one way to find out who's home," Tate said, starting down a gravel trail that led from the road to the house.

Stephanie didn't waste any time in following him. When they reached the house, they stopped to listen. Luca slipped around the back, returning after a few moments with a report. "All closed up tight. Shutters are drawn, but someone's been here recently."

Stephanie gasped. "How do you know?"

"There's a half-burned newspaper out back. Looks like someone had a campfire going. Date on the newspaper is three days ago."

Tate held up a hand. "Did you hear that?"

Luca and Stephanie froze.

"I didn't hear anything," Luca said. "What?"

Tate listened for another long moment before shaking his head. "Nothing I guess. Just my imagination."

Stephanie approached the door. "Enough wasting time."

Both men protested, but she shrugged them off. "A woman at the door is less intimidating," she said.

"Depends on the woman," Tate murmured, his mouth quirked in a half grin. Luca and Tate took up positions on either side of the door as Stephanie knocked.

"Eugene? My name is Stephanie. I wanted to talk to you."

No sound came from inside the stone house.

"I'm not here to bother you. I just have a quick question."

No response.

She put her hand on the door and turned the handle. It gave slightly. "It's unlocked," she mouthed.

Luca shook his head and put out an arm to stop her from entering.

"We've got to," she whispered.

This time both Tate and Luca moved to stop her as she pushed open the door. They stood frozen as it swung wide with a low groan. The interior was dark and cool. Stephanie could make out a tiny living room with a rocking chair and a rickety shelf overflowing with books of every shape and size.

"Eugene?" she called again. "My name is Stephanie. I need your help. My father's in trouble. I'm going to come in so we can talk, okay?"

This time both Tate and Luca pushed in front of her and entered first. Biting back both fear and irritation, she followed them in. The house was perfectly quiet. A shadowed hallway led to the kitchen, and she followed Tate into the cramped space.

Tate tried his best to keep Stephanie behind him. At least he was able to ascertain that no one was in the kitchen before she pushed in. The yellowed tile counter was immaculate, in complete juxtaposition to the round table, which was covered with feathers, each fixed to an index card with a pencil sketch of a bird.

He picked up one and looked close. "Guy's a good artist," he whispered.

Stephanie tried a light switch with no result before she opened the refrigerator. "It's empty. No electricity."

Tate pointed to a cooler under the table. "Low-tech fridge."

She pulled open the lid of the cooler and perused the supplies floating in half-melted ice. "Water, and jars of peanut butter and jelly. Eugene lives simply."

Luca called them back out to the living room. "No one here. Bedroom's got nothing in it but a sleeping bag tossed over the box spring. No sign of a car, so I wonder how he's getting around."

"Even my trailer looks cushy compared to this," Tate said. "Hard to believe this guy's been in possession of a priceless violin all these years. Why hasn't he sold it? Maybe we got the wrong info."

"I don't think so," Stephanie said, picking up what looked like a small bar of soap. It was scored and scratched across the surface. "Violin rosin."

Tate held up a hand. "Quiet. Hear that?"

They froze, and a faint creaking sounded faintly.

"He's here somewhere," Tate mouthed.

"There's a closet in the bedroom, but I checked," Luca said, voice low. "It was empty."

"Eugene is probably better at hide-and-seek than you are," Stephanie whispered to her brother.

Tate headed for the bedroom, which was, as Luca described, bare of personal effects, save for the worn sleeping bag. Luca caught his arm.

"I didn't shut the door."

Now the door was firmly closed. Tate wrapped his fingers around the handle and counted to three before he wrenched it open. Eugene was not there, only a set of three empty hangers and a knitted cap tossed onto a wooden peg. One of the hangers moved ever so slightly. A waft of cool air hit Tate's face. Looking in the back, he saw the source—a small door hidden in the back wall, which had not been fully closed. It opened with a creak of old wood, exposing a tunnel.

Tate took a penlight from his pocket and immediately plunged into the gloom, followed by Luca and Stephanie. The old tunnel had a cement floor and walls covered in broken brick. Thick wooden beams were lined up every four feet along the ceiling, hanging with cobwebs that trailed into the gloom. Tate had to stand bent over to avoid bashing his head on the low beams.

Their eyes adjusting to the darkness, they moved forward, Stephanie stumbling and falling to her knees. Tate helped her up, momentarily pulling her body against his, feeling her warm breath on his neck, the silken caress of her hair. Her hands squeezed his biceps for a dizzying second while she regained her balance.

"Thanks," she said.

*My pleasure,* he thought, remembering how he'd used to hold her in his arms every day, then how he'd thrown her away along with his own happiness. Shaking the feel of her out of his head, he moved along, wishing they'd thought to bring a flashlight. The space grew narrower as the tunnel pinched in, the air stuffy and dank. He jerked in surprise as a drop of cold water landed on his neck from one of the rafters overhead.

"Must be an underground spring close," Luca said, swatting at a cobweb that clung to his face.

"This is old. The original home owner must have wanted his own private exit."

"Or he was storing something down here that he didn't want the world to see," Luca added.

Tate wondered if the walls were still sound, with the deteriorating powers of water and age working away at them. He inhaled the aroma of dead air. It was the same smell he'd experienced hundreds of times, working shoulder to shoulder with his father. It never ceased to amaze him how solid brick and steel could be reduced to rubble in a matter of moments. A wrecking ball or a series of precisely placed holes filled with TNT or C-4, and a perfectly constructed building could be obliterated. There one minute, gone the next.

A moan echoed through the tunnel, making the hair on the back of his neck stand up.

"Why won't you leave me alone?" the thin voice wailed.

A swaying light blinded Tate until his vision recovered and he could make out the shivering form of the man he guessed to be Eugene, thrown into strange illumination by a lantern he held in one hand. He was slight but tall, his hair long and unkempt, the beard bristling from his chin. His eyes shifted uneasily from Luca to Tate and on to Stephanie.

"Hey there," Tate said, voice low. "I'm sorry if we sca— you."

Eugene shook his head so violently that the lantern li— bounced crazily around the tunnel. "You're not sorry. Yo— here to take it."

Stephanie moved closer. "Eugene, we're not going to — you."

"Those are lies," Eugene whispered, his voice pai— You all tell lies, every one of you."

"No, it's not a lie," Stephanie said. "We're here to — lp my father. I'm sure you can understand that."

"Father?" he cried. "Poor father."

Yes. I'll bet you love your father, too."

—nguish seeped into Eugene's words. "They're gone, — e's gone and I'm alone. I want to be alone. Go aw— n't come back here."

—y don't you tell us who is bothering you?" Luca said. — we can help you."

—way!" Eugene shouted, the cry bouncing off the — inging through the space.

—" Stephanie started, but Eugene was edging back —ness. He must have hung the lantern on a nail — ght was suddenly pinned in place, bringing — n focus.

—Stephanie started.

— dropped as he saw what Eugene clutched in — e knew the power of dynamite. Fuego De— — d a range of explosives over the years, but — ripped was an altogether different beast. — of dynamite made with a mixture of ni— —dust. Relatively harmless—if the blast-

Heart thumping, he looked closer. The cap was still affixed to the eight-inch stick, clutched in the man's trembling fingers.

"Does he know what he's doing with that?" Luca whispered.

"If it's unstable, it may not matter," Tate murmured back. Old dynamite stored improperly would sweat out the nitro, forming crystals on the outside of the sticks, causing them to become highly sensitive to the slightest shock or friction. Dynamite of any kind was dangerous. Old dynamite was deadly and unpredictable. "Eugene, put that down. It's not safe."

"You're not safe. You're here to take it. I have to do it." Tears streamed down his hairy cheeks. In spite of the potentially lethal situation, Tate felt a stab of pity for the man who he realized was mentally challenged and obviously terrified. He had the feeling Eugene had been through his own kind of nightmare. A match flared.

"No, Eugene," Tate said, stepping forward. "Put down the dynamite before you hurt yourself. You can go. We won't stop you. I give you my word." Tate figured they had maybe ten seconds before the match died out.

Eugene shifted, eyes rolling in thought. "I don't know."

Seven seconds left. "You don't want to hurt anyone," Tate said. "I can tell."

Time stood still as the match burned a hole in the gloom.

Five seconds. "I don't want to hurt anyone," Eugene repeated. "But I've got to get away."

The last seconds ticked away.

Eugene touched the match to the fuse.

"Eugene, no!" Tate yelled, leaping forward. Eugene scrambled backward as the fuse caught, tossing the dynamite behind him as he ran. Tate reversed course.

"Run!" he shouted, urging Stephanie and Luca in front of him, toward the entrance, knowing in his heart it was too late.

A deafening boom shook the tunnel, and chunks of debris began to rain down upon them.

# TWELVE

Stephanie lost her footing, sprawling stomach first as bricks smashed into the floor around her. A solid weight pressed down on her, and she realized Tate had covered her back with his torso in an effort to shield her. The world spun around her in a dark maelstrom of noise and choking dust. She felt the secondary impact as heavy rock fell on top of Tate. Sharp bits cut into her cheeks as he pressed her to the cold floor.

The rumbling grew in intensity, and Stephanie feared the tunnel was collapsing around them. They would be buried under tons of concrete, beneath an empty stone house. No one would find them until it was too late. She fought to breathe against the dust and panic.

"Hold on," Tate said into her ear, as if he could read the terrifying thoughts racing through her mind. His hands wrapped around her arms, squeezing some courage back into her.

There was one last groan of protesting wood before the vibrations tapered off, the sound softening and dying away. Debris still poured from above, but it had lessened to a trickle. Tate eased off her. An unsteady light emanated from a burning hunk of wood above them, glowing strangely through the thick curtain of drifting dust. "Tell me you're okay," he said, mouth pressed to her ear. There was such longing in his voice, such tenderness, that her eyes filled with tears. He helped her roll over, and she looked into his dust-streaked face in the flickering light.

"I think so," she whispered, putting her hand to his cheek. He clasped it there for a moment and closed his eyes, breathing hard. It was the same sweet connection they used to share, and it cut to her very core.

"That's my girl," he said.

She could only manage a smile before fear clawed her gut.

"Luca," she cried, trying to scramble to her feet. Tate gripped her arm.

"Move slow. This place is unstable now."

She got to her feet and picked her way through the clots of broken rock. The light was not sufficient to illuminate the dark crevices. She could see no sign of her brother. "Luca?" she called again, her voice shrill. Victor lay broken in a hospital bed, her father was lost and now Luca. It was too much. She would not allow it.

*Give me the strength, God.*

Filled with energy born of fear and faith, she began pushing rocks out of the way, calling her brother's name every few moments. Her back and legs ached with myriad bruises and cuts. With every second that passed, her anxiety edged up a notch until she found herself holding her breath, fingers clenched into rigid fists. "Say something, Luca!" she screamed.

"Here," Tate called from a few feet away. "He's under here."

She waded through the rubble as fast as she could manage. Luca was lying face up under a fallen beam. Tate grunted as he struggled to lift the wood. "Too heavy. Need some leverage."

They looked around for something to use, and Stephanie came up with a long piece of wood, probably knocked loose in the explosion. She shoved it at Tate. He wedged one end under the wood and balanced it over a chunk of cement. "When I lift, slide him out, feet first."

Stephanie nodded, heart pounding.

With an effort that made sweat pour down his face, Tate threw all his weight on the end of the wood.

"It's not moving," Stephanie cried.

Tate did not answer, instead redoubling his efforts, pushing so hard the veins bulged in his neck. Shifting rubble proved that the beam was moving, inch by precious inch, until there was enough clearance for her to haul out Luca from under the beam by gripping him around the ankles.

When he slid clear, she knelt next to him, her cheek to his mouth, checking, praying for a puff of air on her face.

Luca grunted, and Stephanie nearly squealed with joy. "He's alive." He mumbled something else, and she put her head closer to his lips.

"Your hair is in my mouth," Luca said.

She laughed and brushed the debris off his face as best she could. "Are you hurt?"

He shifted as if he was going to sit up, but she held him down. "Not until you answer me."

He exhaled, eyes closed for a moment. "As far as I can tell, I'm okay. I can feel all my limbs and move all my fingers and toes. I might have a concussion...."

"Sounds like a clean bill of health to me," Tate offered.

"Right," Luca said. "Can I sit up now?"

She held his shoulder and helped him ease into a sitting position. Dirt fell from his hair and shoulders. He blinked several times.

"Yeah, everything seems to be working, but my ankle hurts." His eyes scanned the ruined tunnel before they came to rest on Tate. "Thanks for digging me out."

Tate nodded but didn't answer.

Stephanie ran her fingers along his ankle. "Nothing feels out of place, but you might have a fracture."

He eased the ankle back and forth, grimacing. "Just a sprain."

"Uh-huh," she said. "Let's get you out of here, and we can take a look when the light's better."

Luca cast a chagrined glance down the tunnel. "Eugene's long gone, I suppose."

"Yeah," Tate agreed. "But we'll catch up with him." He offered a hand to Luca, and he and Stephanie helped him to his feet.

Luca tried to walk and nearly fell. "I guess I really did mess up my ankle," he grumbled. "Need some ice and it will be fine."

They didn't reply, making their way out. Stephanie exited first, Luca following, awkwardly hopping, using Tate's shoulder for support as he hefted himself along.

When they arrived back in the kitchen, Tate steered Luca to a chair while Stephanie retrieved some ice from the cooler and wrapped it in a towel, applying it to Luca's ankle after they removed his boot.

"It's very swollen," she said. "We'd better get you to a clinic."

"It's only a sprain. It will be fine in the morning."

"Did anyone ever tell you you're stubborn?" Stephanie asked.

"Family trait," Tate murmured, earning a glare from Stephanie.

Luca shook his head. "I didn't think Eugene would resort to dynamite to get rid of us. He seemed harmless enough, but I guess I was wrong about that."

Stephanie wet another towel and used it to dab at a cut on Luca's face before she turned to examine Tate.

He waved her off. "I think Eugene is scared. Maybe he

had a run-in with Ricardo. For whatever reason, he's decided that violin belongs to him."

Stephanie pulled the Polaroid photo from her back pocket and held it to the light from the kitchen window. She shook her head. "I've been focusing on the wrong thing."

"What?" Luca said, wiping grit from his shoulders.

"I've been trying to read the label to authenticate the Guarneri, but there's another way." She held the photo up for them both, pointing to the scroll. "The Quinto has a scar on the scroll from the building collapse, remember?" She peered closely. "It's not definite, but see that mark there? It could be the same scar."

Tate looked at her. "So Bittman is right. The Guarneri really did escape the fire all those years ago."

Stephanie bit her lip. "And it seems that Eugene might be the one who stole it."

"And set the fire to cover his tracks?"

"Bittman said it was another man who set the fire."

Tate sighed. "Ricardo. He's the only other person involved in this besides Maria."

Stephanie nodded, feeling the prickle of fear along her spine. "Ricardo won't stop until he murders Eugene and gets the violin that he tried to steal all those years ago. He killed Devlin because he didn't want Devlin to lead us to Eugene."

Tate sighed. "That leaves us caught between crazy Eugene and a murderer with nothing to lose."

"And don't forget Joshua Bittman," Luca said, voice grim, "a certifiable psychopath."

Tate and Stephanie herded Luca to the car in spite of his efforts to shoo them away, and Stephanie got behind the wheel. It was late afternoon; the sun, low on the horizon, cast long shadows across the road. No one said it aloud, but

Tate found himself wondering how they would track Eugene now, with Luca barely able to walk.

*You're not doing much better yourself.* The pain in his leg was excruciating, aggravated by the extreme effort of hoisting the beam off Luca. He popped two aspirin, knowing it would do nothing more than dull the pain. He thought about the pills in his backpack and how easy it would be to fall back into the numbing narcotic haze. Then, as he had thousands of times in the past year, he made the decision to stay clean and sober. Something tugged at his mind. He thought of the moment the rumbling in the tunnel had stopped, and Stephanie lay still in his arms.

Something called out in his soul that moment, something deeper than his rational thought or his conscious mind. It was the same quiet sense of God stirring, urging him to stay sober every day—the same feeling he got when he sent up a plea for Stephanie's protection today. He was indeed the worst kind of sinner. An addict, a neglectful brother, a man who abandoned Stephanie Gage. Yet in that moment, he found himself again casting his deepest desire up to God for something other than his sobriety.

His every thought for the past year, his every anguished prayer had been dedicated to staying clean. Now his heart seemed to have expanded, allowing him to pray for something beyond himself. The prayer had been answered, and Stephanie was safe. He wasn't sure which was the greater blessing, that she'd been spared injury in a collapse that might have killed them all, or he'd once again surrendered his desires to God—desires that went beyond keeping the pills in the bottle.

He pushed these thoughts back down into the dark recesses of his heart, and bent his thoughts to the task ahead. Maria was still out there somewhere. In trouble up to her neck, no doubt. There had been no messages from her and no leads from Gilly after he had pried into her computer files. What did she think she was accomplishing by trying to take Bittman's violin?

He guided the truck along for another half hour, looking for any signs indicating the direction Eugene had taken. A dirt path, so faint he might have missed it altogether, caught his attention. He tapped the horn to signal a stop and got out, willing his leg not to buckle.

Stephanie joined him, and Luca hobbled up.

Tate pointed to the path. "Could lead to the tunnel exit," he mused.

Luca frowned. "Then again, it could be a hunting trail. Doesn't look like anyone's used it in a while."

Tate shook his head. "I'll check it out. Be right back."

"I'll go, too," Stephanie said. "Luca, why don't you call home and check on Victor?"

She didn't wait for his answer before plunging down the path, which sloped sharply away from the road. The day was hot and the cloud cover pressed warmth down upon them as they pushed past a screen of mesquite shrubs. The wind, which continued to blow, brought no hint of cooling to the sultry air.

Stephanie stopped, listening.

He gave her a questioning look.

"Just wanted to make sure my brother isn't trying to follow. He hates being left out of the action."

Tate hid his smile and pressed on, the uneven ground agony on his leg. Teeth gritted, he continued along, the journey passing in a haze of pain. After another thirty minutes he stopped, under the pretense of checking for broken twigs or marks on the ground. He felt her fingers on his wrist.

"It's your leg, isn't it?"

He shrugged. "I'm okay."

"No, you're not. You're in serious pain. I can tell."

He soaked in her eyes, luminous and gentle. "You get used to it. Doc says this is probably as good as it gets. I can handle it."

She stared, his own face mirrored in her gaze. "How do you handle it? By…" She looked away.

Shame and anger boiled up inside him. "By abusing drugs?"

She shook her head. "That's not what I was going to say."

He put a hand on her cheek and forced her to look at him. "Steph, you never lied to me. Don't start now. You think I'm still using, don't you?"

She gripped his hand and then pulled it away. "I don't want to think so."

"I'm not."

He saw the doubt in her eyes, and his heart broke all over again. The worst thing, even worse than losing her love, was losing her respect. He did not trust himself to speak so he moved ahead, deeper into the tangle of undergrowth. The path was overgrown, and he was beginning to think it was nothing more than an abandoned hunting trail. Then it dumped into a small clearing, crowded by bristlecone pine trees.

A rocky outcropping rose some twenty feet, with boulders piled along the bottom. They moved closer, and Tate was able to discern an opening between the boulders.

Bingo. The exit to Eugene's tunnel.

"At least we know where he came out," Stephanie said. "But how is that going to help us?"

Tate examined the ground carefully, noting a faint set of imprints pressed into the dust. "He's got a motorbike." The tracks led through the grove of trees. They followed on foot to a well-packed path that paralleled the road—wide enough for a vehicle, as least as far as they could see before it twisted away through the trees.

Stephanie wiped her forehead. "We'd better go back and get the cars. We'll never catch up on foot."

"We're going to have to wait until morning."

"No," she said firmly. "There's another few hours of sunlight. We can make headway, sleep in the cars if it gets too dark."

He stood as straight as he could manage. "It's another half hour back to the car, and we're all tired and banged up."

"Then I'll go by myself," Stephanie snapped, eyes flaring, "if you're not in a big hurry to find them."

He tamped down his own surge of anger. "I'm in just as much a hurry to find my sister as you are to get your father back, but one thing I've had hammered into my own thick head these past four years is patience."

She studied his face, and he could see the anger simmer down in hers. A slight smile quirked her lips. "I never would have thought of you as the patient type."

"People can change." *I've changed.* He wanted desperately to say the words aloud, but they refused to cross his lips. Her gaze held his for a long moment before she turned and headed back up the path with no further comment.

Tate did his best to keep up, but it was still three quarters of an hour before they made it back to the car to find an irate Luca. As much as he appeared to chafe at this delay confronting them, he agreed with Tate that a night search after Eugene was foolhardy. They returned to the hotel at sundown, dirty, famished and exhausted.

They picked up some sandwiches from the deli and piled into Stephanie and Luca's room to eat them, debriefing the day's insanity.

"Good news is, we found Eugene, and we can be pretty sure he's got the violin," Luca said.

"Bad news is, we lost him again, and Maria and Ricardo are still at large." Stephanie sighed.

A knock at the door startled them. Tate looked through the peephole. "More bad news," he whispered. "Officer Sartori has come back for another visit."

# THIRTEEN

Stephanie felt her stomach lurch as Tate opened the door. Officer Sartori stood, hands on her hips, looking every inch the cop, even though she wore jeans and a T-shirt.

"Please come in," Stephanie said. "Sit down."

Sartori gave her a thorough once-over. "No need. This will be a short visit. Where have you three been?"

Luca gestured to his ankle, propped on a chair under another bag of ice. "We went looking for the violin, and I had an accident."

Her eyes narrowed. "Uh-huh. I'm not a patient person, as you've probably gathered. Now I'm impatient, and I'm also angry."

Stephanie swallowed. "Why?"

"Because someone high up on the political food chain is pressuring the sheriff into taking me off this investigation."

"What do you mean?" Luca asked.

"The sheriff's getting heat from the county supervisor to direct his resources elsewhere—in other words, he's pulled me from the Devlin case."

"And the supervisor is leaning on the sheriff because...?" Tate said.

"The official line is that we're pulling back to focus on an identity theft ring, so we're leaving the Devlin case up to the Lone Ridge law enforcement, which basically consists of a really hard-working full-time officer and two volunteers who don't have the time or resources for this investigation."

Stephanie willed her feet not to pace. "What's the unofficial line?"

"Are you asking me what I think?" Sartori said.

She nodded.

"I think I'm being pulled off because someone with power and money wants to cover up something. I think that someone has a lot to do with you three and this violin or whatever it is. And you know what else I think?"

The three remained silent.

"I think I'm going to work this case on my own time until I figure out just what Treasure Seekers is really doing in Bitter Song." She pulled a photo out of her pocket. "Do you know this person?"

Stephanie felt her entire body grow cold as she gripped the photo, forcing out the words. "He's a man I used to work for years ago. His name is Joshua Bittman."

"That part I know. I did some digging, and I found out that twenty years ago he claimed his father lost a Guarneri violin. Interesting coincidence that you just happened to be looking for a Guarneri at the moment."

"Interesting," Luca agreed solemnly.

Sartori put the picture away. "Is Bittman the guy you're working for now?"

Stephanie's heart pounded so hard, she thought it would break out of her chest. "We're working on our own behalf."

"Is that right? And when you find this violin, who are you going to give it to?"

Luca cleared his throat. "We'll establish legal ownership and hand it over to the correct individual. For us it's about the find, not the money."

"Well, isn't that big of you? I think I'll have to give Mr. Bittman a call and see if his story jibes with yours."

"No," Stephanie cried out before she could stop herself.

"No?" Sartori repeated, folding her arms across her chest. "And why wouldn't you want me to call him?"

She looked directly into Sartori's eyes. "Joshua Bittman is a dangerous man."

Her eyes narrowed. "I've looked up the esteemed Gage family. Well connected, plenty of money, no legal scrapes pending, no illegal activities under the respectable exterior. So what's this Bittman got on you?"

Stephanie pressed her lips together. Her legs felt as if they were boneless, barely able to support her weight. What could she say that would not result in her father's death? Tate joined her and put an arm around her shaking shoulders. "Officer, we're not the bad guys here, I can promise you that."

Her gaze traveled from Luca to Stephanie and finally rested on Tate. "Okay. I'll leave it for now because I can see you're not going to make it easy on me. That's no problem. I don't like things easy." She opened the door. "But I promise you I'm going to dig up the truth, and I'd better not find out that you're on the wrong side of the law, or I'll make it my mission in life to lock you up. Am I making myself clear?"

"As crystal," Luca said.

"You can expect to be seeing me in your rearview mirror. I'll be your personal shadow while you enjoy the finer things in Bitter Song." She smiled. "Have a great day."

Sartori left, and Stephanie's legs would not hold her up anymore. She sank down on the bed, sucking in a shaky breath. "If she calls Bittman, he'll kill Dad."

Luca hopped over and sat next to her. "He wants the violin. If we can convince him we're close, he won't hurt Dad."

Stephanie knew that deep down, Luca was just as scared as she was. "Call Tuney. Maybe he's found out something."

She focused on breathing, keeping herself calm while Luca dialed, putting Tuney on speakerphone.

There was a clatter of noise on Tuney's end.

"Where are you?" Luca asked.

"Clinic. Got a lead on your dad. Followed it to an apartment, only someone was waiting and I took a bullet to the shoulder."

Stephanie gasped. "Oh, no. Tuney, are you okay? You could have been killed."

"I'm fine. Your father was being kept there, I think, but they moved him."

She felt like screaming. "We've got a cop here who is onto the truth. She's going to contact Bittman."

Tuney grunted. "Then I'd better pick up the pace over here."

"We can't ask you to risk your life," Stephanie said, choking back a sob.

"You're not asking. Talk to you soon." Then he was gone.

Stephanie closed her eyes, head spinning. "This is all going wrong."

Tate took her hand. "I think we need to call Bittman. Tell him we're close. Buy ourselves some time to find Eugene."

Stephanie gripped his fingers, trying to stem the panic flowing through her veins. "I don't think I can talk to him without losing it."

"I'll talk," Luca barked, picking up her phone.

"Luca…" Stephanie started as he punched in the numbers.

"I know what the stakes are, sis." He listened for a few moments, frowning. "He's not answering." Luca spoke to the answering machine. "We've located the man with the violin. We'll pick him up tomorrow, and you'll have your prize. We'll turn it over when you return our father." He clicked off.

"So what do we do now?" Stephanie asked.

"We try to get some sleep," Tate answered.

*And count the minutes until morning,* Stephanie thought.

Tate stretched out in the camper of Gilly's truck and fell into a restless sleep, interrupted by the pain in his leg. Stephanie had argued with him to let them pay for a room until she'd run out of breath. He awoke hours later, disoriented, to find it was still dark, his watch showing a few minutes after four in the morning. Lying there, willing his body to come awake, he listened, trying to figure out what had awakened him.

A soft crunch made him bolt upright. The sound came from the rock pathway that skirted the small hotel. He pulled a corner of the curtain aside and peered out. A sliver of moon did little to illuminate the area. Holding his breath, he stared intently into the darkness.

A flicker of movement from the bushes alongside the building caught his eye. Pulling a T-shirt on over his jeans, he didn't bother with shoes. Slinking into the front seat, he tried to ease open the driver's side door without making any noise. His plan fell apart when the creak of the metal hinge sounded loud in the predawn. Throwing caution aside, he leaped from the vehicle and barreled into the bushes.

There was a muffled exclamation and a cry of surprise as he wrapped his arms around the figure, holding tight.

"Stop it, Tate."

He was so surprised by the voice that he let go, and his sister climbed to her feet.

"You big dummy. You could have killed me."

"Maria?" He didn't know which emotion to act upon. He settled for a hug of profound relief. He squeezed her to his chest and rocked her back and forth. "I'm so glad you're here." He pulled her to arm's length and looked her over thoroughly. "Are you okay? Are you hurt?"

"No, I'm not hurt," she whispered, brushing the leaves

from her hair. "No thanks to you." She looked around. "Let's sit in the truck. More private."

Mystified, he followed her to the truck. She sat in the passenger seat, darting nervous glances out the window.

She took a deep breath. "I can't believe this is all happening."

He frowned. "Did you come here to find Bittman's violin?"

She twisted her long hair between her fingers. "Yes, that's how it started."

His frustration boiled over. "Why would you do something like that? You know what kind of man Bittman is."

"I didn't," she fired back, eyes gleaming. "I thought he loved me. At first he was really nice, and I thought we were…" She broke off and wiped a tear from her face. "Never mind. I can't undo any of that. Please don't rub it in my face."

She was right. It was not the time for blame. "Okay. I'm sorry. I was just crazy with worry about you."

She pressed her fingers to her temples. "So why did you and the Gages come here anyway? Just to find me?"

He took a deep breath. "Not just for that. Bittman kidnapped Wyatt Gage. If Stephanie doesn't find the violin for him, he'll kill Wyatt."

Maria's dark eyes rounded in shock. "He's a monster."

He squeezed her hand. "You aren't to blame for that."

She shook her head, eyes wet. "I didn't listen. Stephanie tried to tell me, and you did, too, but I didn't listen."

He took a deep breath. Maybe they could salvage things before they got any worse. "Let's focus on getting you out of this situation. Tell me why you decided to go after his violin in the first place."

"That's not important. The point is I did, and when I got here I found out I wasn't the only one looking for it. This guy named Ricardo was spying on me when I was with Bittman, and I think he followed me to Devlin's shop."

"Bittman's pool guy."

She nodded. "He met me as I was leaving the shop and convinced me we could find the violin faster if we worked together, and we could sell it and split the money. He said the Guarneri belonged to his great uncle or something, and Hans Bittman stole it from him. He's been working under-cover at Bittman's to turn up any leads. I believed him." She shot Tate a look. "Was that another dumb mistake?"

"Finish the story. What did you and Ricardo do next?"

"We contacted Devlin. He said he could get a picture of the violin, but when I went back, he wasn't there. Devlin had told me about the guy who came into the shop with it, so I started asking around. Somebody pointed me to Bitter Song, and I came here and found the man. His name is Eugene."

Tate tried to keep down his growing excitement. "So do you know where the violin is right now?"

"I think it's with Eugene. I've been visiting him, gain-ing his trust." She flushed. "So we could get him to tell us where it is."

"But he hasn't so far?"

"Not yet. Ricardo said Eugene was a thief, the vagrant who took the violin from the music store years before, but…" Her forehead wrinkled. "The more I talked with Eugene, tried to gain his trust, I found out he's really sweet. Confused and scared, but not the cutthroat guy Ricardo made him out to be. I'm supposed to meet him up at the ruins in two days."

"What ruins?"

"A ghost town called Lunkville, north of Eugene's stone house. When I get the violin, I'm to contact Ricardo to meet me there." She shook her head. "I thought it was a good plan, but now I'm not sure anymore. That's why I came here, to talk it out with you. It doesn't seem right to take it away from

Eugene. He doesn't care about the money, and I'm sure he didn't know it was wrong when he stole it from Bittman." Her voice hardened. "Bittman doesn't deserve the violin anyway, if his father took it from Ricardo."

Tate took Maria's hand. "Listen to me carefully, Maria. Ricardo is not who you think he is. His family never owned the violin. We think he set fire to Bittman's shop all those years ago and killed Bittman's brother, Peter. As soon as he gets his hands on that Guarneri, he's going to kill Eugene and probably you."

Her eyes widened in fear. "No. That can't be true."

He squeezed her fingers. "I'm not lying to you. You know that."

She sucked in a breath, and her eyes filled with tears as she yanked away her hand. "Oh, no. What have I done? How could I have made such a mess of everything?" A trail of tears flowed down her face.

His heart constricted at the misery in her eyes. "You made mistakes. We can fix it if you let me help."

"No, Tate. This time it can't be fixed." She was sobbing in earnest now. "What would Dad say if he could see me now?"

Tate's breath caught. It was a thought he'd entertained a thousand times through his own struggles. What would his father say to see his son addicted to pills? His relationship with Stephanie ruined? Fuego Demolitions facing bankruptcy?

"He would say you made a mistake, and he would forgive you." Tate felt a swirl of comfort speaking the words aloud, and at that moment he knew he needed to believe it as much as his sister. "Listen, Maria. You got off track when Dad died. You started looking for love, and you thought Bittman could give that to you, but he isn't capable of it. Lesson learned. It's my fault, too. I should have been there for you, and I wasn't. I'm sorry."

She shook her head, wiping her face with a tissue. "I can't wish it away that easily." She turned a tear-streaked face to him, vulnerable as a child's. "Oh, Tate. I'm scared."

"I'm not going to let anyone hurt you."

"What about Eugene? Ricardo will find him and kill him."

He raised his voice over her rising hysteria. "Not if we get there first."

"We? I can't involve you and Stephanie any more than you already are." She looked at her lap. "Or Luca, especially after I accused him. Tate, I lied about him. I wanted him to like me, and when he didn't, I lashed out. He was never anything but kind to me." Tears started again. "My life is a wreck. I'm so ashamed."

"Honey, we all have things we're ashamed of, but God forgives all of it, just like Dad said." He was startled at his own words. He recalled that it had been the first step on his road to recovery, asking God to forgive him and make him whole again. It felt good to put that into words for Maria, at long last.

She stared into his eyes. "Do you believe that?"

He smiled and caught her tear on his finger. "You know, I think I really do."

Maybe people couldn't forgive. He thought of the distrust in Stephanie's eyes, the anger in Luca's.

But God could.

She sniffed. "I came earlier to talk to you, but I saw a woman here so I left. Who is she?"

"Cop."

Maria started. "What did she want?"

He hoped his words wouldn't drive Maria further into despair. "She's investigating the murder of Bruno Devlin. He was run down the same night we found you in the shop."

Even in the weak light, he could see all the color drain out of her face. "Oh, no. Ricardo told me that he had some business to take care of." She bit her lip. "I think he went back and killed Devlin so he wouldn't tell Bittman we were getting close to his violin. He's a murderer." Her voice fell to a whisper. "I've been helping a murderer."

"You didn't know. You couldn't have." He checked his watch. "It's almost five. I'm going to wake up Stephanie and Luca. We'll make a plan to get to Eugene before Ricardo does." He got out of the truck and went around to the passenger side.

Maria rolled down the window, anguish written plainly on her face. "Tate, I'm sorry I got you into this mess."

He stroked her cheek. "Hey, there. Don't beat yourself up. Fuegos are famous for making messes, but we always clean them up, right?"

She didn't answer, so he leaned in to kiss her on the cheek. "Stay right there. I'll be back in a minute."

Maria nodded, and he trotted to Stephanie's door. A knock at five in the morning was never good, and he knew they were both dog tired, but he had the sense that every moment wasted left a greater window for Eugene to disappear—or worse, for Ricardo to get hold of him before they did.

Stephanie opened the door in seconds, hair mussed, eyes smudged with fatigue, and still the most beautiful woman he'd ever seen. He swallowed the sudden onslaught of emotion at the terror he'd caused her with his early morning intrusion. "Sorry to wake you."

"I wasn't sleeping."

"Maria's in the truck."

Her mouth opened. "Is she okay?"

"Yeah. She's set up a meet with Eugene day after tomorrow. We can intercept them."

Stephanie gasped and immediately turned to wake Luca. "Bring her in. Let's go over the details."

He trotted back to the truck, something like hope beating

in his heart. They'd turned a corner, finally. His sister was safe for the moment, and maybe, just maybe, they could get Bittman's violin back before Ricardo tried to kill Eugene.

As he neared the car, the hope was replaced by a growing dread. Maria was not in the front seat—only a scrap of paper and a note scrawled in pen.

*I'm sorry. I'll fix it. I love you. M*

"Maria!" he yelled, heedless of whom he might bother. He ran in the direction he thought she must have taken. There was no sign of her. He kept searching anyway even though he knew it was hopeless.

Eventually he returned to the truck and banged his fist against the side.

He looked up and saw Stephanie standing there, understanding in her eyes. She knew it, too. Maria was going to walk right into Ricardo's hands, and it would destroy any chance of saving her father.

# FOURTEEN

Stephanie felt like screaming. One step forward and three steps back. She plopped down onto the battered chair and pulled up on her laptop some satellite maps of the area while Tate related Maria's confession. She could not fault the girl entirely—after all, she'd been unable to discern Bittman's true nature as well, but now the morass was deepening, and if things didn't change, none of them would get out of it alive.

"In order to get to this ghost town," she said, "I'm thinking we should follow the trail from Eugene's house that we found yesterday."

Luca considered. "Makes sense. We may even find Eugene along the way if he stopped to camp."

"Agreed." Tate's mouth was still tight with frustration, though. He looked like he was about ready to explode.

Luca was unable to suppress a groan as he tried to put weight on his damaged foot. "I'll be okay."

Tate and Stephanie exchanged a skeptical look.

"Come on," he growled, limping to the car.

Stephanie pointed to a section of the map, and Tate peered over her shoulder. "Looks like Lunkville is down on the sand flats, maybe about three hours from here. It's an old railroad town, or what's left of it." She looked at Tate. "How is Maria planning to get there?"

He shrugged. "I don't want to think about it. She's resourceful, and she thinks she's going to fix everything. I just hope she doesn't hitch a ride and get into even more trouble. She's stubborn."

Stephanie shot him a look. "Family trait?"

He didn't reply, instead turning to Luca and shoving his hands into his pockets, his brow furrowed.

"Luca, Maria told me that she accused you of...pressuring her when it wasn't true. It was wrong of her to do it." He took a deep breath. "She's sorry, and so am I."

Luca didn't speak for a moment. "I guess if it came down to it, I'd take my sister's side, too."

Tate rubbed a hand over his eyes. "She's not a bad kid, just insecure. After Dad died, things only got worse. Too much happened all at once, and she can't get past it."

A hint of a smile lit Luca's face. "That can keep a person stuck in one spot, all right."

Stephanie saw the wistful expression in Luca's gaze, and she knew he was thinking of another woman, a woman he'd loved and lost. It brought Brooke to mind, the woman deeply in love with Victor, and her heart ached. The Gage family had had their share of trials, too.

"Anyway, I'm sorry," Tate said.

It had never before occurred to Stephanie how difficult it was to say those two words, or how hard it was to accept them. He'd tried to apologize after the accident, but she had turned away, sickened by his addiction and deeply hurt by his abandonment. If Bittman hadn't taken her father, she might never have seen Tate again. It would be the easy way, but for some reason she knew it would not have been right. They needed to clear the air between them so they could both start their lives fresh. She would not allow herself to love him again—but maybe it could be a tenuous bridge between them, unsteady though it might be.

If they could somehow climb out of the present mess.

Luca clapped Tate on the shoulder. "Forgotten. Let's move on and get to Eugene."

They hurriedly packed up bottles of water and the left-over sandwiches from the night before. They had another surprise waiting when Tate tried to start the truck. Several turns of the ignition using the key yielded no results. It took him another minute to find the reason. He groaned. Maria had ripped away the ignition wires.

Tate got into the back of the rental car, his face a mixture of anger and amusement. "Good thing you didn't leave yours unlocked, or she would have disabled it, too."

Stephanie allowed herself a smile. "At least she didn't steal it."

"She probably would have if I didn't have the keys in my pocket," Tate grumbled.

As they rolled to the edge of the parking lot, Stephanie driving and Luca in the passenger seat, Rocky the janitor jogged up, broom and cell phone in hand. "Call for you," he said, thrusting the phone through the window.

Stephanie thanked Rocky and took the cell, her stomach clenching into a knot. "Hello?"

"I'm okay, little lady. Don't let him…"

She sat forward, electrified. "Daddy! Has he hurt you? Tell me where you are."

"He is unharmed for the moment," Bittman said, coming on the line. "But I am losing my patience. This investigator, Tuney, he is causing some inconvenience to me."

Stephanie was unable to answer, her father's voice still ringing in her ears.

Luca took the cell and jabbed the speakerphone button. "If you hurt him, it will be the last thing you ever do."

"Such bravado, but we've no time for this. I have had to intervene with the local authorities already. Another annoyance. I thought I spelled out very clearly that you were to stay away from the police."

"Sorry, but there's been a murder here," Luca snapped. "Cops don't turn a blind eye to that."

"The music store owner." Bittman's voice was thoughtful. "It proves me right."

"About what?"

"Whoever burned down my father's store is after my violin, and he's eliminating any potential witnesses. Perhaps he'll eliminate Maria, too. I surmise they are working together."

"Enough," Tate shouted.

"Aah, the oaf is there with you. Stephanie, you are worthy of so much more. You were better off without him."

"Stop it," Stephanie hissed. "I want to talk to my father again."

"I've no more time to waste, and neither, it seems, do you. Call off Tuney, or I will be forced to kill him. Keep the cop away, or she will also meet with an accident. And find my violin. Quickly. I'll tell your father goodbye for you." He hung up.

Luca snapped the phone shut, and Stephanie held it out the window to the waiting Rocky.

"How does he know where we are?" Stephanie managed. "I haven't seen anyone following us." Her voice shook.

"Doesn't matter." Tate shifted impatiently on the seat. "We've got to get moving."

Luca took out his own phone and reluctantly dialed Tuney's number, then left a message. "I doubt he'll give it up. You know Tuney."

Stephanie shivered. She could not bear it if something happened to Tuney.

She eased down the driveway and headed out of town, keeping an eye on the rearview mirror. She wasn't sure who she was looking for. Ricardo? Sartori? Maria? Alternating waves of panic and rage swept through her. Tate's face in the rearview was grave, Luca's tired, haggard and tinged with pain. It all came back to her decision long ago to work for Bittman, to let him into her world.

He'd permeated her life like a toxic gas, enveloping the people she loved the most: her father, her brothers and Tate.

The thought startled her. Not Tate. Not anymore. She shot a look at him again.

*"...past is passed, just like you said. Supposed to be forgiven, right? That Christian thing?"*

Could she forgive Tate for the hurt he'd heaped upon her? For the stupid choices he'd made when he'd fallen into addiction? For shutting her out?

Something shifted inside her, like a sheet of ice breaking to reveal a pool of water underneath. Maybe she could forgive him, and reconcile herself to his continuing addiction, if indeed he was still using.

But she could not love him.

Not again.

Pressing harder on the gas pedal, she aimed the car away from town, toward the yawning desert.

Tate clamped down on his rage toward Bittman and tried to decipher the map Stephanie had printed as they retraced their route to Eugene's. The highway shimmered before them, basically flat except for gentle swells and dips. The road on either side stretched out in endless miles of sandy ground, covered by a scalp of low bushes. Mountains rimmed the horizon in the distance, scraping their peaks against a sky so blue it hurt to look at. Under other circumstances, it might have been beautiful.

Wind buffeted the car as they drove, easing only slightly as they took the turn to the stone house. He was relieved to see no sign that any recent vehicles had disturbed the dust around the structure. At least Ricardo hadn't made it there— not by car anyway.

Tate let himself into the house to do a quick check, in case Eugene had returned. He hadn't, but Tate made an interesting discovery that he shared with the others.

"Peanut butter is gone from the cooler. I think Maria made a stop here before she took off."

"Could have been Eugene," Luca said. "Maybe he came back, changed his mind and headed off in another direction."

"Nope, it was Maria."

Luca raised an eyebrow. "Why so certain?"

"Because she hates jelly, and that was left in the cooler." Tate climbed back into the rear, and they drove once again to the trailhead they'd found the day before. His leg was not as painful as it had been, but the memory of his conversation with Stephanie was every bit as uncomfortable.

*How do you handle it? By abusing drugs?*

She thought he was an addict.

She thought right—he was and always would shoulder the risk of using again.

But he would never touch another narcotic as long as there was any life left in him.

That's the part she didn't know.

He would die before he allowed himself back into that abyss.

Stephanie eased the car down the slope, the sides scraping against the bushes that crowded in from either side. The jostling tossed them around, and Tate could tell it wasn't doing Luca's ankle any favors. Just when the trail pinched in to the point where he thought they would have to stop, they emerged at the exit to Eugene's tunnel.

On the other side of the clearing, the narrow road climbed sharply as it wound through the trees, and he wondered how far they would be able to go in the car. With Luca's ankle injured, they would not cover much ground on foot.

Wind scattered leaves across the windshield, and Stephanie clutched the steering wheel in concentration. The makeshift road sloped downward through a canyon speckled by crystal-flecked outcroppings of rocks. Minerals colored the cliffs in stripes of gold and red as they reached the bottom and began a gradual ascent that took them to the top of the canyon and out onto an inhospitable landscape of rock and sand.

Stephanie slowed as they took in the barren panorama. "What's that?"

Tate looked in the direction she pointed. A small ridge in the distance marked the edge of a ravine.

She was already unbuckling. "We can get a look at what's below." She had to heave the door against the wind.

"Steph…" he started, but she was already marching resolutely, hand shielding her eyes against the flying grit.

Luca unbuckled his belt and made to follow her.

"I'll go," Tate said. "Rest your ankle."

"It's fine." Luca grimaced. "Just a sprain."

Tate was about to reply when a movement on the horizon stopped him. Behind Stephanie, starting from the far edge of the plateau, a massive cloud of sand began to form, a gigantic chimera rising from the desert floor.

"Sandstorm," Luca breathed, pushing at the door. "Stephanie!" he yelled as he struggled out of the car.

"Stay here. I'll get her."

Luca shook him off. "No, she's my sister."

Tate grabbed him by the shoulders, his face inches from Luca's, yelling over the wind, which had begun to howl. "You can't help with your ankle like that. Get back in the car." He didn't wait to see if Luca would follow his commands. Instead he took off, sprinting after Stephanie.

He saw her stop and turn, her face tilted toward the monster bearing down on her.

He tried to call her name, but the huge tower of sand sent out a wild shriek that swallowed up his voice. The wind was screaming now, bearing down on them both with speeds that must have topped fifty miles an hour. They could not outrun it.

His brain understood, but his legs did not.

*Get to Stephanie* was all he could fathom over the roar of the storm.

Forcing his body to move through the blasting wall of sand, he kept on.

The most serious risks from sandstorms, he knew, were suffocation and blindness from the airborne avalanche of sand. He tried to put it out of his mind as he pushed ahead, nearly falling as the ferocious blast forced his weight on to his bad leg. Grains of sand cut into his face, pricking at his eyes, causing them to tear up.

He fell, struggled back to his feet and fell again.

"Stephanie!" he yelled. She was no more than twenty feet away now. "Get down!"

She might have shouted something back, but he could not hear it as a wall of moving desert closed in around them, and he lost sight of her.

# FIFTEEN

One moment Stephanie was surrounded by clear blue sky, and the next, she was enveloped by a massive cloud of stinging sand. Tate appeared just before the storm swallowed her up, and then he was gone, overtaken by the undulating cloud. She began to cough, gasping for air as stinging particles flew into her mouth and eyes. She wanted to run, but she no longer knew which was the way back to the car and which led to the edge of the ravine.

She covered her nose and mouth with her elbow and ran blindly anyway, panic fueling her flight. Anything to escape the painful suffocation. Sand and grit cut her cheeks, and the wind hammered against her. Suddenly a pair of arms wrapped around her legs, bringing her to her knees. Tate.

Tate wrapped her in a bear hug, and they pressed their faces together as the storm howled around them. Somewhere in the back of her mind, she realized he was wearing short sleeves, leaving nothing to shield him from the onslaught, so she pressed closer, lifting her arms and trying to cover them both with her jacket. A sudden shock sent them tumbling as a branch careened by them, powered by the wind. They clung together as the storm crashed over them and a cocoon of sand piled up around their bodies, sifting into their hair, looking for entry into their noses and eyes.

Pounded by the wind, Stephanie lost track of time. *Just hold on,* she told herself, tightening her grip as much as she could around Tate. She felt a second sharp impact as an object, perhaps another branch or rock, ripped from the ground and hit home, knocking the breath out of her. The rage she felt against the storm, against Bittman and even Tate, gave her the strength to fight, but even that strong emotion ebbed against the power of the wind-frenzied sand.

*I won't let go.*

Her clawed fingers began to lose their hold, and she felt herself tearing away from Tate.

"No!" she yelled, and tried with every bit of strength she had left to hang tightly to him. He was strangely passive in her arms. "Tate!" she yelled.

He did not answer, nor did he stir in her arms. A cold chill of fear crept into her body.

"Hold on!" she screamed again. Was it her imagination, or was the gritty cloud beginning to lighten?

The wind hammered with such violence that in spite of her most heroic effort, he began to slip from the circle of her arms.

She tried to grasp him under the shoulders, but he was pulled away.

"No!" she yelled again, mouth filling with grit as she threw herself on top of him.

Just as her hold began to fail, the storm passed, whirling away into the ravine.

The silence was shocking. The only sound coming from her was labored breathing and the hammering of her heart. She spit out a mouthful of sand before sucking in as much fresh air as she could hold.

She let go of Tate and sat up, blinking the sand out of her eyes, shaking it from her ears and unloosing piles of it from her jacket.

"I can't believe we made it," she said, coughing and shaking more sand.

Tate lay on his stomach, unmoving.

For a moment, she could only stare in horror.

"Tate?" He was so still. She could not see the rise and fall of his chest. Crawling over to him, she gently turned him over. His face was covered in blood, seeping from a wound on his forehead where something had struck him. She tried to brush it off with her sleeve, but there was so much—a crimson tide that ran down his neck and soaked into his shirt.

She ripped off a piece of her shirt and balled it up, pressing it onto the wound.

He still did not move.

She looked frantically for Luca, who was nowhere in sight. Her phone was back in the car where she'd left it.

Terror rose inside until she could not form a coherent thought. She pressed her mouth to his neck.

"Please do not leave me," she whispered, fingers trying to find a pulse.

Her trembling fingers would not obey.

"Tate," she whispered, her tears dropping onto his face, etching trails onto his dusty skin. "Tate, Tate, Tate" was all she could manage, tracing her fingers over his head, his cheeks, the curve of his chin, the hollow of his throat.

She could no longer feel the ground under her or the wind, suddenly gentle, that toyed with her hair. She pressed her lips to his, desperate to feel an answer there. He remained motionless. The last of her strength left her and she put her face to his chest, tears soaking into his ruined shirt.

She felt movement as he inhaled deeply. Jerking to her knees, she stared into his face as his eyes slowly came open, confused and disoriented.

"Tate?" she whispered.

"You okay?" he mumbled.

She could only fight to control her cascading emotions as the gray eyes cleared and he struggled to sit up. He tried to get to his feet, but he toppled over. She tried her best to keep his head from hitting the ground. She rolled him onto his side and pressed her face to his cheek.

"Stay still, just for a minute," she whispered into his ear. Holding him around the shoulders, crouched next to him, her cheek touching his, an overwhelming current of some deep emotion flowed between them. She was transported back in time, past the anguish of addiction, the pain of being shut out. She thanked God again that Tate was alive. It was truly the only thing that mattered.

Tate clutched her hand in his, and for that brief second she wondered if the past was erased for him, too. It was Tate and Stephanie again, facing the journey ahead together, their back turned on the ugly road they'd already traveled. Did he feel it as strongly as she did?

A shout from the direction of the car broke the spell, and Stephanie got on her knees to find Luca hobbling up, using a stick for support. "Stephanie!" he yelled again.

She waved both arms to show him that she was unhurt and turned her attention again to Tate, who had now raised himself to a sitting position.

"I think I took a rock to the head," he said.

Stephanie reined in her emotion and forced a grin. "Won't do it any harm. You always said Fuego craniums were made out of cement."

"Plywood," he corrected.

She gave him her arm to help him get up, and he leaned against her briefly as dizziness overtook him. "You probably have a concussion. We'll take you to the hospital."

"Not likely," Tate said. "Let's go. We've already lost too much time. Besides, Maria might have been caught in the storm, too."

He straightened and headed tentatively back to the car, Luca and Stephanie staring after him. Luca examined Stephanie closely. "I tried to call for help, but there's no signal up here. Not sure who I would have called anyway."

She rolled her shoulders. "He should go to the doctor."

"But he won't," Luca said. "He's as stubborn as I am."

She shot him a look. "Yes, but I guess we're all guilty of that character trait. We'll bandage him up as best we can, and I'll watch closely in case he really does have a concussion." She could just make out his tall frame, limping slightly on his way to the car.

Had it all been imagined, the warmth between them—a by-product of trauma? How could he still have such control over her emotions, this addict, this ruined man who had meant everything to her? She felt angry at herself for imagining feelings that didn't exist.

Luca put a hand on her shoulder. "You sure you're okay?" he asked.

She nodded. "Scraped up is all."

"You look strange, like you just discovered something."

"What would I discover in the middle of a sandstorm?" she snapped. She felt Luca's eyes on her as she walked to the ridge to take a look, now that the storm had passed.

Tate allowed Stephanie to fuss over him with the first-aid kit because he knew she wouldn't agree to leave otherwise, and it gave him time to get himself together. He still felt confused. One moment he was plunging through a wall of sand, and the next, lying with Stephanie at his side, stroking his cheek, murmuring something unintelligible in his ear. He was sure he'd imagined the longing he heard in her voice, the tenderness that made his breath grow short, even now, as she wiped the blood from his face and affixed a bandage to his forehead. He didn't want to experience the strange warmth that coursed through him and sent him off balance. The strange disequilibrium eased a bit, though the pain in his leg flared anew, and now his head throbbed, too.

She avoided looking into his eyes, muttering something about hospitals and stitches. Then she got behind the wheel, though he tried to edge her out.

"I'm the only able-bodied one around here," she said. The engine coughed to life, and they continued on. "It looks as if once we get across these dunes, there's another road—a trail, more like. It heads in the direction of Lunkville, according to the maps I downloaded."

Tate let her talk while he kept his eyes trained for any sign of Maria. He prayed she'd not been caught by the same sandstorm. More and more, he felt the urgency to extract them both from the mess that brought Stephanie back into his life. The violin was the key—find it, and maybe everyone really would get what they needed. He hoped it was quick. He did not understand the intense feelings that he'd experienced over the past few days. It felt like he was standing on dangerous ground, the sand shifting under his feet.

Luca tossed down his phone in frustration. "Useless until we get another satellite link."

Stephanie approached the end of the plateau, which fed them through a narrow gap between two massive rock cliffs. "What were you researching?"

"Emailing back and forth with the retired cop who handled the music store fire." Luca rubbed at a spot on the window. "He told me Ricardo's last name is Williams. He worked at Bittman's store, doing odd jobs and janitorial stuff. That must be how he saw the Guarneri and decided to take it for himself."

Tate tried to forget the dull ache in his head. "Why set the fire, though? Why not just run with the violin?"

"He probably figured it would slow down the investigation and give him time to vanish."

"Which he did," Stephanie added. "For twenty plus years. Last laugh was on Ricardo when he burned down the shop but didn't get the Guarneri."

*Last laugh's going to be on us, if he gets his hands on it now,* Tate thought.

"But Ricardo never stopped looking for it. He must have been keeping tabs on the music world, too. When he heard Bittman was on the trail, he tried to get close, worked as the pool guy even." Luca laughed. "Bittman's gonna have a conniption when he figures that one out."

It gave them all a small sense of satisfaction, Tate knew, to think of one way Bittman had been fooled.

The rock cliffs pinched together until there was only a passage barely wide enough for one car. As they crawled toward the gap, trees poked through the earth with limbs twisted and shorn off by the untamed wind.

Stephanie rolled down the window, checking the clearance on the driver's side. Tate did the same out the passenger window.

"Going to be a tight squeeze." She pushed the hair out of her face.

"Not as tight as the Manhole." He wished immediately that he hadn't said it. A flush colored her cheeks petal pink, and his own face warmed. He remembered the situation in perfect detail, recalling it from time to time in his happier moments. It was their first foray into spelunking at a cavern in Gold Country back before the accident, before everything had gone bad. She'd pushed ahead into the darkness broken only by their headlamps, teasing him about being too slow, and shimmied into a hole dubbed the Manhole by cavers over the years. Stephanie had promptly found herself wedged in. While others might have panicked, Stephanie laughed until her face was wet with tears while Tate crawled around to the other side of the hole and yanked her out by the ankles. He'd called her Pooh Bear, after Winnie the Pooh's famous "stuck" scene, for months afterward. They'd enjoyed reliving the memory perhaps more than the actual trip.

*Stick the memories back in the past where they belong, Tate.* There was only pain in recounting his time with Stephanie. She'd moved on, and he could not blame her.

Stephanie poked her head out the window again and eyed the sides of the car. Tate did the same. No more than a few inches clearance, but it would be enough if the path didn't narrow any further. He reached out and snapped off a twig of a spiky shrub to examine it closer. Freshly broken, as were many others.

"Someone's been this way recently," he said.

Stephanie flicked a glance at him. "Eugene?"

Tate shook his head. "He was on a motorbike. I don't think he'd have caused this much damage."

"Maria?" Luca suggested.

"Hope so." Tate didn't want to think about the other possibility—that Ricardo had already passed by, killed Eugene and taken the violin. A sudden movement along the rocks made them all straighten until Tate caught site of the source. "An animal, ground squirrel I think. Wait a minute—do you hear that?"

Luca stiffened in the backseat. "There's a car following."

"I'll check it out." Ignoring Stephanie's protest, he climbed out the window since there was not enough space to push open the door. Scrambling onto the rocks, he climbed upward to the nearest flat one, where he could get a look at the path they'd just traversed.

The vehicle was leaving the sand flats. He caught a glimpse of a dark-colored truck before it began to climb the slope. It moved slowly but steadily, vanishing into the tree-covered incline that would lead right to them.

He returned to the car and crawled back inside. "Truck. Don't recognize it."

"So we have a decision to make then," Luca said. "Move forward and get to Eugene, or stop and find out who's behind us."

Tate rubbed at his throbbing head. "We've tried the waiting thing already. I say we go. The window of opportunity to save Eugene and this violin is small."

In silent assent, Stephanie started the car forward, the sides scraping against overhanging branches. They climbed another hundred yards before they reached the pinnacle. Out the back window the truck was visible, winding its way through the same sunbaked route.

"Closing the gap," Luca said. "Can you push faster?"

Stephanie tightened her grip on the wheel and stepped harder on the gas. Gravel pinged against the undercarriage as they traversed a hill that looked down onto another seemingly endless plateau of corrugated ground, cut through by cracks filled with dry grass and creosote bushes. There was no sign of any human habitation as they took the last turn before entering the flatlands. Stephanie rounded the corner and slammed on the brakes, but not quickly enough to avoid the improvised spike stick, a narrow strip of wood bristling with nails. One front tire rolled over the stick with a loud pop that sounded like gunfire.

The car lurched slightly, the rear wheels skidding to one side.

Tate was out immediately. "Front tire is blown. Do we have a spare?"

"One," she said with a groan.

He looked around. A rock-strewn slope behind them, and in front, miles of sunbaked nothing. Behind, he heard the relentless approach of the oncoming truck. They had only a few minutes, not enough time to change the flat.

He felt the wild surge of reckless energy from days gone by.

"Okay," he said. "Here's what we're going to do."

# SIXTEEN

Stephanie's heart thundered in her chest as she crouched behind a rock, looking down on the road below them. Luca sat behind the wheel in their car. She didn't like it. He was vulnerable, and though he was one of the toughest people she knew, he was injured. If the person in the truck was Ricardo, he could walk up and fire a gun into the driver's side.

Her mouth went dry, and she tightened her grip on the soccer-ball-size rock she'd eased to the edge of the slope, praying Tate's desperate plan would work. Her eyes watered as she peered across the bleached landscape, trying to spot where he'd gone. In spite of his leg and the head injury, he had quickly disappeared into the rock maze after he'd helped her shimmy the rock into place and tuck herself out of sight.

The truck was close now. She could see the glint of sun on metal as it approached the final curve. She leaned forward slightly, hands pressing the rock. The truck pulled to a stop.

Her fingers were slick with sweat. She blinked against the dazzle of the sun. Was it a man behind the wheel? A woman? She could not tell. Leaning forward, she braced to shove the rock down the slope if the driver turned out to be Ricardo. It would provide a momentary distraction only. She prayed a moment would be enough for Tate to gain control of the situation.

The door of the truck opened and a figure got out, hair covered by a baseball cap, untucked plaid shirt over worn jeans. Then she saw Tate edging out of hiding, just behind the driver.

Pulse pounding, she leaned forward. The sandy soil underneath the rock gave way, and the weight of stone carried it to the road below. Both Tate and the stranger looked up at exactly the same moment.

Stephanie's breath caught. "Look out!" she shouted.

Tate grabbed the arm of the driver and yanked. The rock sailed by, across the path and down into the ravine below.

Stephanie scrambled down from her hiding place as Luca shot from the car.

"It's Officer Sartori," she called, too late.

Tate helped up Sartori from the ground. "Sorry," he said. "We thought you were somebody else."

Sartori glared at the three of them, brushing the dirt from her clothes. "You were expecting Ricardo Williams, maybe?"

Stephanie sighed. True to her word, Sartori had been researching the case in spite of the sheriff's order. "We weren't sure."

"Uh-huh." Sartori looked over their rental car. "Somebody left a little booby trap for you? Could be miners. There are still a few old-timers around, looking for that big gold strike."

Stephanie shrugged. "Are you following us?"

"Maybe. It's my day off. Would have intercepted you sooner, but I caught the tail end of a sandstorm." She eyed Tate's bandaged head. "You, too?"

"Yes." Stephanie pushed the thought of the storm firmly away. "But we're okay."

"Why are you headed out here? Lunkville's this way, but it's nothing but a ghost town."

Stephanie knew there was no use trying to hide information from Sartori any longer. She sucked in a deep, shuddering breath. "We got a lead that a man named Eugene is in possession of the violin and he's come this way."

"Eugene? Guy with a wild beard?"

"Yeah." Luca leaned on his good ankle. "Know him?"

"Not well. Moved here about five years ago, I think. Took up at the stone house, squatting really, since it belongs to some city guy who hasn't lived here in twenty years. Eugene's got mental problems, but he's pretty harmless. We don't hassle him because he doesn't make trouble. Just wants to be left alone." She raised an eyebrow. "So he's got Bittman's violin?"

"We're not sure." Tate pointed to the flat tire. "Could be he left us this present. I've got to change it."

Sartori shrugged. "I'll give you a hand, but you're going to have to follow me back to town, I'm afraid."

Stephanie shook her head. "No, we can't do that. We've got to check out Lunkville and see if Eugene is there."

"Nope," Sartori said. "I don't think so."

Stephanie felt a prickle of annoyance, but she kept a level tone. "We've been through a lot already, and we're not giving up now. We haven't broken any laws, and you're not technically supposed to be following us anyway."

Sartori held up a hand. "Different issue. The reason I drove up here was to give you a message. Rocky called me from the hotel and said he couldn't get you on the phone, but he'd heard you talk about where you were headed."

Tate cocked his head. "What message?"

"From the hospital," Sartori said.

Stephanie felt as if the ground shifted under her feet. The word *hospital* unlocked the terror inside her that seemed to whiz around her head and heart, creating a buzz so loud she could hardly hear herself ask the question. "What is the message?"

Luca stepped up behind her and put a firm hand on her

shoulder. Tate looked at Stephanie with a mixture of worry and fear written on his own face. Frozen in a terrified tableau, they waited for the words to come.

Sartori's face softened. "I'm sorry to be the bearer of bad news, but your brother Victor has developed a blood infection."

"How bad?" Stephanie whispered.

Sartori shifted uncomfortably. "Seems as though he's spiked a fever they haven't been able to control." She cleared her throat. "They suggested the next of kin should be present."

*Next of kin.* Her head spun, and her legs began to shake until Luca guided her to the car so she could lean on the back bumper. The rest of the conversation seemed to come from a distance.

"There was a follow-up message from a Brooke Ramsey." Sartori cleared her throat. "She said she contacted the pastor of your family church."

Luca peppered her with a list of questions ranging from what time the call had come in to airport information. Sartori fielded the questions patiently. "I'll help change that tire and give you all a moment." She busied herself working with Tate to hold the lug nuts when he loosened them.

Luca embraced Stephanie, but she felt no comfort from it. Victor was not going to make it. They could not save him. Just like they were unlikely to save her father. She felt sickened and numb.

"...the next flight," Luca was saying.

"I'll go with you to the airport," Tate answered. "Then I'll come back and continue the search."

Tate and Sartori labored together to replace the ruined front tire with the spare. They worked in silence, the only sound coming from the clank of the lug wrench and the murmur of Luca on Sartori's satellite phone as he inquired about flight information.

She sat on a rock, the heat seeping into her, yet not warming the cold place deep inside.

*He's won. He's killed Victor, and he'll kill Dad, too.*

From the moment she'd walked away from Joshua Bittman, she'd feared something like this would happen. He was interested only in acquiring everything he desired, and the means to that end were unimportant. He would get his violin, without their help if it came to that. With Victor and her father gone, she knew he would not stop pursuing her, stalking her, watching her. She flicked a glance at Luca and Tate. If anyone else got in his way, he would take care of them, as well.

She felt the bitter taste of defeat. Nothing she'd done since the moment she'd learned of Victor's accident had made the slightest difference. After a while she felt Luca's hand on her shoulder again. "There's a flight out in three hours. We can just make it."

She stood up, looking over the vast sprawling vista below. No matter where she went, how deeply she buried herself, the past was still there. Bittman was still there, as sure as the sunset.

"Let's go, Steph."

She squeezed her eyes closed. *Lord, I got myself into a mess, and only You can help me get out of it. Heal my brother and give me the strength I need.* Something rose inside her, not courage exactly, but a feeling she'd forgotten in the recent crush of events—the feeling that she wasn't alone, and God would walk with her through the desert like He'd always done. "No," Stephanie heard herself say.

Both men stared at her.

She stood up. "Luca, you go back. Be there for Victor and Brooke. I'm staying here, and I'm going to get that violin. It's the only chance left for Dad."

Luca grabbed her fingers and squeezed until she looked at him. "We'll keep looking for Dad. Tuney and me. You need to come with us, for Victor." He shot a glance at Tate. "We'll help you as much as we can from back there. I can ask some buddies of mine to come and search for Maria."

Tate didn't answer.

"I'm going to help Victor my way, Luca. It's my fault he's in that hospital. It's my fault Dad's with Bittman. I can't help either of them in San Francisco. The only thing I can do is stay here."

"No," Luca said.

She looked him full in the face. "I'm staying."

He opened his mouth, anger and resignation warring there. "You need to be with Victor, in case…" His voice broke, and at that moment her heart did also.

"I'll be praying every moment," she whispered to him, clutching his hands.

Luca cleared his throat. "It's not safe to leave you here alone."

"I'm not alone. Tate will stay here with me."

Tate remained silent, but gave a slight nod.

Luca looked at her again and gave her a fierce hug.

Fighting tears, she hugged him back, the pain in her heart almost too much to bear.

Tate could not think of a single thing to say to help the situation. He watched Luca kiss his sister once more as she got into the car, head bowed, lips moving. It was probably the hardest decision she'd ever had to make, to stay behind when her brother was likely to die. If there was something he could do, anything to ease the anguish on her face, he would do it in a heartbeat. The only thing left was to find the violin, find his sister and save her father's life.

Luca drew him aside as Sartori got into her truck and

started the engine. His eyes were shadowed with fatigue and pain. "So it's on you now," he said, eyes glittering. "I'm sorry to leave things like this. It's dangerous and…"

"And you don't trust me," Tate said flatly.

Luca exhaled. "I guess I don't have a choice." He looked away for a moment. "You've shown me someone different through this whole treasure hunt, though, a Tate I didn't know before."

Tate felt a sudden thickening in his throat. He was different; at least he desperately wanted to think so. He settled on a nod.

"But you're not good for Stephanie. You tossed her aside and messed her up so badly that she went to work for this psycho."

The truth cut into him. Nothing had really changed at all because in Luca's mind and Stephanie's, he would always be locked in the past, bound so tightly to his sin that he could never be free.

"We'll get the violin," he said.

Luca gave Tate an appraising look. "I know you care about her enough to keep her safe, so I'm going to have to rely on you to do so, but that's it." Luca stared at him. "She's better off without you, and she knows it. I don't want to be cruel, but I've got to watch out for her, like you would for Maria."

He nodded. She was better off without him, probably always had been. "I'll take care of her."

Luca offered a hand. His grip was crushing. "I will hold you to that." They locked eyes until Luca let go, hobbling to the truck without a backward glance. Tate got into the car. Stephanie did not protest when he took the wheel. Sartori walked up and handed them a handheld radio and a folded paper through the driver's side window.

"It's a satellite radio. It will work even if your phone doesn't. I think the paper is a bill or something from the hotel. Rocky was afraid you were going to skip out, I think. Probably figured you for criminals, due to my frequent visits." She checked her watch. "I'll be back up here after I drop off your brother and take care of a few things."

"To arrest us for something? Trespassing in Lunkville, maybe?" Tate asked.

Sartori grinned unexpectedly. "Maybe. Or maybe I'll just tag along for the treasure hunt. You all are sort of growing on me."

Stephanie gave her a wan smile. "It's dangerous. People who hang around me—" she swallowed hard "—have a tendency to get hurt."

"Then I'll bring Bear," she said. "Bad guys have a tendency to get hurt around him, too." Sartori returned to the truck and backed down the trail. Stephanie waved, fingers trembling, face pale, until they were out of sight.

Tate could not stand her stricken look. He took her hand, pressing some warmth back into the cold fingers. "We'll find the violin. I promise."

She bit her lip and forced a deep breath. "What did Luca say to you back there?"

Tate shook his head. "Nothing I didn't already know," he answered, gunning the engine to life.

They followed the road down, scouting ahead for any more spike sticks, but there were none. Arriving at the bottom, they continued on for what seemed like an eternity. The late afternoon was warm, the air that rushed in through the open windows sultry and pine scented. Stephanie spotted the turnoff toward Lunkville.

"There. It's overgrown, but that's got to be it."

There was no way to tell on the rocky entrance to the trail if any other vehicles had passed there recently. He took it slow, easing over the uneven ground. The last thing they needed was another flat, especially with no spares left. Under the sparse canopy of a Joshua tree were the ruins of a log cabin, roof slanted crookedly and windows long gone.

He pulled the car to a stop and got out, intending to check it out before Stephanie joined him. But true to form, she made it to his side before he did so. The interior was dark and smelled of rotted wood as they peered through the window gap.

"Empty?" she breathed in his ear, tingling the skin along his neck.

"Looks that way." They entered, picking their way carefully to avoid the places where floor planks had caved in, revealing dark recesses underneath. He inhaled, catching the tang of something unexpected.

"Cigarette smoke," he said.

Stephanie nodded. "Maria doesn't smoke, and there was no sign that Eugene did, either."

Tate had a sudden flash of memory. When he'd tangled with Ricardo in the alley, he'd filed away an important detail in his memory. Ricardo had had a distinct odor about him—the acrid smell of cigarettes.

# SEVENTEEN

In the next several miles there were four more structures in various states of decay. One was a mere shell with walls, a few ruined fireplace stones and a small windowless jail. The others had been homes and the remnants of a building, which Tate decided must have been some sort of garage. Over time the airborne grit had scoured the paint off the sides and worn away the edges of shutters and railings, as the desert inexorably reclaimed the town. None of the buildings revealed any clues or hiding places where Eugene or Maria might be holed up, but most held the faint scent of cigarettes. Hours passed before they had completed their search and stopped to rest, sweaty and tired.

Leg and head throbbing, Tate climbed to the top of an old steel tower and surveyed the surroundings.

"Looks like the rest of the town is clustered in the hollow about a mile from here," he called down to her. "There's a railroad track just beyond the hill." He eyed the sky as he climbed down. It was dusk, and the sky was darkening, rapidly cooling the air around him.

Stephanie looked at him. "I know what you're thinking. We should wait until morning."

"No, I was thinking we should rest, eat something and wait until dark."

Her eyebrows lifted in surprise. "Really?"

He almost smiled. "Really. Ricardo is here so we've got no time to waste, but if we go marching into town while it's daylight, we're sitting ducks." And truth be told, he desperately needed to regroup if there was to be any kind of physical encounter in the next few hours.

He let her lead the way to the car, so she wouldn't see how badly he was limping. She retrieved a bag and handed him a sandwich and some water. They sat in the car and ate greedily, gulping down the water in spite of its warmth.

"It's another two hours until sundown, and we'll tack on one more to be sure it's dark." He got out of the car.

"Where are you going?" Stephanie asked.

"To rest in the cabin over there. Didn't look like any critters call it home."

She cocked her head. "You can lie down in the backseat."

"Nope."

"Why not?"

"Because you need to lie down in the backseat." He finished off his water bottle. "See you in a few hours. Lock the doors and keep the radio close, just in case."

She grabbed his sleeve. "Wait. Here." She pressed something into his hand.

He looked down and found a bottle of aspirin in his palm. "Am I limping that badly?"

"Yes. And I know you don't have…"

"Have what?" The realization dawned on him. "Painkillers."

She flushed.

He pulled his arm away. "Listen to me, Steph. I don't use anymore. I told you I didn't, and I was telling the truth."

"But I saw them in your backpack."

He closed his eyes and bit back a groan. "Yeah. I keep them there. You know why?"

She shook her head.

"Because every day I ask God to help me keep that bottle closed, and every night when the lid is still on, I know I beat it. Every single day, I beat it with His help." The anger throbbed in his throat, the injustice that he would never be clean in her eyes. And he wouldn't allow himself to become any more vulnerable around her.

*You're not forgiven, not by Luca and not by Stephanie. And you never will be.*

She might have called out to him, or it could have been the mournful sound of an owl winging its way over the darkening landscape. He did not turn. He could not. She would look at him through eyes filled with bitter memories, and he could not stand to see it on her face. Instead he settled into a corner of the old shack and tried to sleep.

Stephanie stretched out on the backseat, eager for sleep that did not come. She wondered if Tate was able to get any shut-eye. The angry scene replayed in her mind.

*Because every day I ask God to help me keep that bottle closed...*

*Every single day, I beat it, with His help.*

She felt conflicted by his outburst. Day by day, he was beating back the addiction that nearly ruined him. The strength it took to do that, she could not imagine. But addicts often lied, didn't they?

They did, but something in Tate's gray eyes told her that he was not lying. Besides, of all the things he'd done to her— shoved her away, blown up when she'd tried to stop him from using, forbidden her to work for Bittman—he'd never lied to her.

Never.

She let herself entertain the incredible thought. What if

he was clean? Would there be a chance at reconciliation between them?

For a moment, her heart felt light, dancing on an ethereal hope until the dark feelings took over again. Memories trickled across her mind, stinging like crawling insects.

Tate bleary from the drugs. *Let go of me, Steph.*

Her grasping desperately at his arm. *You can't drive. I won't let you.*

*I don't want your help. I don't need it. I don't need you.*

Those words had hurt more than any of the rest.

*I don't need you.*

She'd made up her mind right then not to need him, either. Ever. In spite of what her aching heart told her, the emptiness of her arms was a feeling to be pushed aside and buried deep.

*I don't need you, either, Tate Fuego, and I never will again.*

She prayed for Victor then, hands clutched so tightly her fingers ached. With no chance of sleep, she powered up her laptop, scanning emails to find one from Tuney. There wasn't one, and none from Luca, but she chalked that up to the inconsistent wireless connection. She checked her watch. Luca was probably just landing in San Francisco. Her heart throbbed again thinking about Victor.

She shut down the computer and shoved her hands in her pockets to ward off the chill that was settling in as the temperature dropped steadily. Her fingers found the paper from Rocky. He'd been helpful and kind. She was not sure what gave him the idea they'd skip out on paying the bill.

She unfolded the note. It was a printed copy of an email sent to the hotel.

*Please forward this message to Stephanie Gage, without delay.*

*Stephanie, as it is September 20th, the anniversary of the date I first met you, it was my pleasure to send flowers to the hotel, the deepest azure, the color you wore upon our meeting that day. You were not there to receive them, I have been informed. Please call me with all haste and report on your progress. When you have found my violin, we will celebrate. Devotedly, Joshua.*

She bit her lip to keep from screaming. Flowers. She used to love them, but now every blossom reminded her of Joshua—the parade of bouquets sent to her for the anniversary of their introduction, her birthday, Valentine's Day. She felt sick. It had started out so innocently. She'd been referred by a client of her father's to do a computer consulting job for Joshua. There should have been some sign in his pale countenance, some hint of madness in his eyes, but she had seen nothing to give her pause until much later, until it was far too late.

She tapped out a message on her phone, anything to keep him off her back for a few hours longer so he would not take action against her father or Tuney. *Getting close, S.* Without much hope that she could communicate a message from such a remote location, she hit the send button.

The hours passed in agonizing slow motion. Finally, when the stars showed against a brilliant black velvet sky, she let herself out of the car, pocketing the keys and putting Sartori's radio in her back pocket. Tate met her in front of the cabin.

"Get any rest?" she whispered.

"No. You?"

"No. That bill from Rocky was actually a message from Bittman." She relayed the contents. Though she could not see his face, she felt him stiffen next to her. Something made her take his arm for a moment. She felt a flood of guilt that she'd kept such a hard heart, that she hadn't believed he was finally clean. "Tate, you were right about Bittman. I should have listened to you."

He sighed, a small sound filled with the same wistfulness she felt twining through her own emotions. "Lots of people fall for his charm. I just hope we can keep him out of this before anyone gets hurt."

"He seems to know my every move," she said as they started up the winding trail.

"This time we're going to get there first." Tate pushed ahead of her. "We'll stick to the rocks as much as we can. Radio?"

"Got it."

He pressed something into her hand, encased in a hard leather sheath. "Your knife?"

"Yeah, just in case."

She pushed it into her other back pocket, and they crept along past the ruined buildings that cast otherworldly shadows in the moonlight. They found the broken railroad tracks and used them to guide them into what had once been Lunkville, a thriving town supported by the productive borax mines.

Tate stopped to let her catch up. "There," he said, pointing suddenly to a lopsided building in the distance. "I saw something, a flicker of light."

She held her breath, staring until her eyes burned. "I don't…" A gleam of light shone for an instant before it vanished again. Tate was already crouched low and moving fast, keeping to the shadows as much as he could. She jogged behind him, pulse pounding.

They pulled up even with the building. There were a half-dozen windows that Stephanie could see, but all of them were too high to peek through. Tate edged his way around the ramshackle structure and she followed, avoiding some of the beams that protruded like splintery claws. They found themselves at a back door, pulled crookedly closed, the handles rusted through. Tate flicked on a flashlight and cupped his hand around it to dull the light.

"It's been opened recently," he whispered, peering at the marks in the earth. "I can't make out any footprints. Contact Sartori on the radio and tell her what we're up to."

"No time," Stephanie said. She grasped the corrugated handle and heaved, the whine of distressed metal thundering through the air before she darted inside, Tate at her heels. Her eyes struggled to adjust to the near darkness. Moonlight shone dimly through the gap where a window had been. The interior of the cavernous space was filled with oxidized mining equipment, all coated by a dull layer of grit. She turned on her own flashlight and pointed it to the floor. Footprints shone distinctly in the grime.

Stephanie saw her own surprise mirrored in Tate's expression. He held up two fingers.

She nodded. There were definitely two sets of prints leading to the rear of the space. Walking carefully to avoid tripping over the odd collection of antique equipment, they moved farther into the darkness.

Stephanie felt the aching mixture of fear and hope. The footsteps were mismatched, one large and one smaller. It had to be Eugene and Maria. Anticipation rose inside her. Ricardo might have given up, left Lunkville without his precious violin. She held her breath as they approached an enormous rusted cart, which she surmised had transported loads of borax ore to the waiting trains decades before. Now it crouched like some prehistoric animal waiting to devour them. The smell of mold tickled her nose, and she caught a musky scent of animal, as well.

Tate pulled her to his side, forcing her to come to a stop. She stood in the shelter of his arm, motionless except for the blood that raced through her body. A soft swooshing echoed through the building. Above them? From behind the cart? She could not tell as the sound bounced wildly.

She turned sharply as the noise intensified; skin prickling, as she tried to pick up the origin. Tate aimed the beam of his flashlight at the rafters far above. The light caught dozens of beady eyes staring, a column of skittering mice traversing the beams above them. Ears twitching, they surveyed the trespassers down below.

Stephanie gritted her teeth, trying not to think of the living freeway of rodents right over her head. If one dropped down onto her, she was not sure she could prevent herself from screaming.

Tate kept hold of her hand, and she clutched the strong fingers. Her tension mounted as they edged by the cart, giving them an unobstructed view of the rear. Piles of rotting boxes stood along the wall in what had once been a tidy arrangement. Now they had spilled through the ruined cardboard, disgorging their reddish contents onto the floor.

Stephanie's breath hitched as she viewed the outline of a door. It probably led to a smaller storage area. They both saw the gleam of light at the same time, a slight glimmer under the threshold.

Tate let go of her hand and moved stealthily to the door until his foot caught on a discarded length of chain. He kept his footing, but the chain scraped against the floor. There was a scuffling beyond the closed door. Tate turned to look at her just as the door crashed open. Eugene, eyes wild in his tangle of hair, tore out of the storage room, clutching the straps of his backpack.

"Wait," Tate called, but Eugene pushed by him, knocking him into the pile of boxes.

Tate righted himself and took off after Eugene. Stephanie overcame her shock to join in the pursuit when she heard something inside the storage space. Fearing it was Ricardo, she drew back into the shadows.

"Tate?" a voice whispered, soft and tremulous. "Is that you?"

With a surge of relief, Stephanie hurried inside. "It's Steph, Maria. Tate is here, too. He went after Eugene."

Maria was huddled in the corner, her face luminous in the dark. She clicked on a small lantern that blinded Stephanie for a moment.

Maria's long, dark hair was pulled into a loose braid. She wore a torn pair of jeans with an oversize shirt. There was a rolled-up sleeping bag in the corner, along with the remains of a box of crackers and a half-empty bottle of water. "You found me."

"It wasn't too hard. We knew where you were headed. How did you get here?"

Maria shrugged. "Thumbed a ride from a guy who mines for turquoise. I gave him my watch in exchange. I guess I'll never be on time again," she said with the ghost of a grin.

Stephanie's tension boiled over, and she could not restrain her impatience. "We've been chasing you for days. Why did you decide to go after Bittman's violin?"

Maria's face went sullen. "I loved him, at least I thought I did. He led me to think we were going to be married, but then he changed his mind. I realize now he never really loved me at all."

Stephanie didn't voice the truth. *He didn't. He isn't capable of it.* "He's got my father and…" Her voice failed as she thought of Victor.

Maria moved closer, and Stephanie could see honest regret in the lines around her mouth. "I'm sorry. I'm truly sorry. I had no idea he would force you into helping him." She paused. "Or maybe I did know, deep down. Our last fight was about you. I sneaked into his office and found a whole display

of pictures of you. It was almost like a shrine or something."
Her eyes flashed. "I told him that things had to change now—
he had to let go of his sick fascination with you."

Stephanie closed her eyes. "He'll never let me go," she
whispered.

"That's what he told me. Then he threw me out."

Stephanie's anger ebbed away, leaving a numb horror in its
wake. "Maria, I'm so sorry. I didn't see the truth about him
at first, either. I wish I'd never introduced the two of you."

She shook her head. "Doesn't matter now. I knew that his
precious violin had surfaced. It seemed like the perfect way
to get back at him and start a new life."

"But Eugene didn't want to part with the violin, did he?"

"No. That doesn't matter anymore, anyway. Tate told me
that Ricardo is a murderer, so I came to warn Eugene." Her
eyes glimmered in the lantern light. "He's a bad guy. Eugene
said Ricardo was here in Lunkville, sniffing around. We decided to wait it out here until he left."

Stephanie noticed a window, one pane of glass broken and
the rest glazed with dirt. She walked over, stood on a crate
and peered out, looking for any sign of Eugene or Tate. "Did
Eugene have the violin with him? Was it in his backpack?"

Maria laughed. "You know, Eugene is a little slow in some
ways, but he's as crafty as they come."

"How's that?"

Maria walked over to the corner and pushed the backpack
aside. She loosened a floorboard and pulled something out
of the space below. Grinning, she held the violin case in her
hand. "Tate is chasing after a guy with a backpack full of
peanut butter and jelly."

Stephanie felt a surge of relief so strong that it almost
brought her to her knees. Sucking in a breath and fighting
back tears, she managed a smile. They'd found it, the one

chance to save her father's life. She took a step toward Maria, when suddenly a gunshot exploded through the air.

Stephanie watched in horror as Maria crumpled to the filthy floor.

# EIGHTEEN

Tate sprinted after Eugene until the man came to an abrupt stop at the mouth of what must have been a mine shaft. It was covered over with weathered boards, except for a V-shaped gap. Eugene stood with his face to the wood, one trembling hand pressed there. Tate reached out and tugged the ragged hem of Eugene's shirt, causing him to whirl around. His eyes were round, mouth open to suck in gasping breaths.

"He's here, he's here," Eugene wheezed.

A gunshot rang out.

Only one, and the night slipped back into silence.

Ricardo? Had he found Stephanie? Tate's mind wheeled between the echoing sound and the man before him. "I need the violin, Eugene. Please."

"No. It's mine. I have to keep it safe." He stabbed a dirty finger at the warehouse. "From him."

Tate moved forward as Eugene eased back.

"Where did you hide it, Eugene? Is it in your backpack?"

Eugene shook his head violently. "It's in a safe hiding place, with a friend."

Tate felt his gut tighten. "Your friend is a girl, right? With dark hair? Her name is Maria, and she's my sister. If you gave her the violin, then someone is after her, too. Is that what you want?"

Eugene's eyes clouded, shifting from Tate's face to the warehouse and back to Tate.

"Go back," he whispered. "She's in there."

Tate looked toward the building where he'd left Stephanie, where his sister might very well be holed up. Eugene used the moment of hesitation to disappear into a gap between the boards covering the entrance to a defunct mine shaft.

Stomach twisted in terror, Tate left off his pursuit of Eugene and ran as fast as he could over the uneven ground, back to the warehouse. All the while he tortured himself with thoughts of what had happened. He'd left Stephanie behind, with Ricardo somewhere close by. If she was hit… Her perfect face rose in his memory, laughing eyes, glinting with life, heart filled with lion-size courage. She could not be dead. He would not allow himself to think it. Nor would he imagine similar things happening to Maria.

He pushed faster until he pulled up at the back door, panting and shirt damp with sweat. It had been opened, the mark of booted feet showing clearly in the loose dirt. Moving as quickly as he dared, he retraced the route they had followed moments before, stopping every few feet to listen. He thought he caught the echo of a shoe on the hard floor.

Stephanie. His heart pounded a frantic rhythm, and he prayed with every step.

*Please keep her safe.*

Even though her heart would never belong to him again, he knew at that moment he would lay down his life for hers.

*Just hang on, Steph.*

From outside the building, he got the crazy notion he'd heard a helicopter somewhere close by. Maybe Sartori had returned like she'd promised, with reinforcements. Hope burned hot in his gut.

There was a blur of movement from behind a pile of rusted metal. A bullet cut through the air by his head. He threw himself to the ground, belly first. Another shot followed, ricocheting off the metal cart and pinging upward, sending the mice swarming in all directions along the rafters. His breath disturbed swirls of dust on the ground, and he tried not to inhale.

"Hey, boy," Ricardo called out. "Didn't think you'd make it."

Tate looked around, knowing that the longer he stayed in one spot, the easier he would be for Ricardo to shoot.

"You are not going to take what's mine," Ricardo growled.

Tate scooted under the cover of a tower of dilapidated wooden crates, his mind racing. He had to get to Stephanie, and the only way was to keep Ricardo talking until he could figure out how to take him down. "The violin isn't yours. You tried to steal it from Hans Bittman. It never belonged to you."

Ricardo snorted. "I did the work, I planned the theft. I even burned down the building to cover it up, and then what do I find?" Ricardo snapped out the words as Tate kept moving, now ducking behind a deteriorating steel barrel. "Some homeless guy runs off into the woods with the Guarneri, and I'm left with an empty case and arson on my plate."

"And murder," Tate yelled. "Don't forget the fire killed Peter Bittman, and it was you who killed Devlin, wasn't it?"

"Yes. I wanted him to tell me about Eugene, but he refused. Things got out of hand." Ricardo laughed. "I'll give you points for persistence, boy. I thought the spike stick would slow you down until I finished up here."

"You let Eugene slip away with the Guarneri. Bad mistake."

"The violin is mine!" Ricardo roared. "I will have it back."

"And then what?" Tate asked, trying to get a fix on Ricardo's location. "You'll kill Eugene because he witnessed you set the fire all those years ago?" There was no answer, and Tate stared into the darkness, his nerves screaming. "Well, now there are more people who know the truth. You can't kill us all."

The chilling silence lingered, and then Ricardo's reply came from somewhere above Tate. "Oh, yes I can, boy. And I will," he heard, just before the tower of crates crashed down on top of him.

Keeping low, Stephanie tried to tend to Maria, whom she had dragged behind a stack of palettes. She'd done her best to secure the door, wedging a piece of wood under the jamb. If Ricardo climbed through the window, there was not much she would be able to do about it, but the window was small and it would be an awkward entry.

Breath coming in pants, she held the flashlight close to the whimpering Maria. Tears streaked the girl's face.

"It's okay. Let me see where you're hurt."

"My side," Maria moaned. "Oh, Steph. Is it deep?" Abject terror shone in Maria's eyes, and Stephanie raised her shirt as gently as she could. The wound was just below the ribs, and though Stephanie was no nurse, she did not think it was deep, but rather a shallow laceration caused by the bullet grazing her. A hole in the back of the garment told her it had passed through. She breathed out in relief.

"It's not bad," she said, taking off her jacket to tie around Maria's waist in an effort to stop the bleeding. As she did so, her fingers grazed the soft swell of Maria's belly. The truth dawned on her in one blinding flash. Maria was indeed trying to start a brand-new life, but not just for herself.

"Maria, are you…?"

Maria's eyes locked on Stephanie's and she nodded, a fresh flow of tears painting trails on her dirty face. "I thought he would be happy, but he didn't want the baby. He kicked me out and called me a tramp. I was going to get us a fresh start."

Stephanie held Maria's hand, swallowing her sadness

at Maria's clumsy attempts to take responsibility for her unborn child. This poor misguided girl was going to be a mother, if they made it out alive. The stakes had just risen even higher—if that was possible. "It's okay. It's going to be okay." There was the thump of a booted foot on the door.

Maria let out a little yelp.

"Open up," Ricardo barked. Maria and Stephanie froze in terror.

"I'm coming to get my violin."

Stephanie looked around frantically for an exit. There was no back door, and the window would be impossible for Maria to climb through since she'd been shot.

A fist slammed into the door. "I've got plenty of bullets and lots of time. Open the door, and I'll make it quick for both of you."

Stephanie raced around the small room, thinking there had to be something she'd overlooked, something they could use to defend themselves, when Ricardo pushed through the door. Tate's small knife would be useless against a gun. Searching desperately for some sort of hiding place, her eyes were drawn to a square cut into the floor. It was the faint outline of a trapdoor.

Her eager fingers found an indentation that must have served as a handle. She yanked on it with all her strength. At first, it did not budge. Then with a groan, it came loose and Stephanie hauled it upward. The space below was ink dark and cold—some sort of basement, she guessed.

She hurried back to Maria. "I'm not sure it will help. We could find ourselves trapped down there with no way out."

"It will buy us some time," Maria whispered. "Until Tate comes back."

For a moment she thought she heard the sound of a helicopter, but she could not be sure over the pounding of her heart. She felt a thrill of fear picturing Tate walking into the warehouse with Ricardo lying in wait, but she could think of no other option. Returning to the edge of the opening with the flashlight, she saw a sloping set of stairs. "Can you manage it, Maria?"

Maria was already crawling toward the opening, one hand clutching the violin case. After a moment to steady themselves, Stephanie started down first, her flashlight making only a minuscule dent in the oppressive darkness. Cobwebs brushed her face, and she thought about the hundreds of mice she'd seen earlier. Putting them firmly out of her mind, she tried to support Maria, who clung to her arm as they made their unsteady way down fifteen steps, testing each one gingerly first. Mercifully the wood held, and when they got to the bottom, Stephanie raced back up the steps and pulled the trapdoor closed from the inside. There was no way to lock it. Ricardo would find them, but perhaps not right away.

What would happen to Tate? As she rejoined Maria, she suddenly remembered Sartori's radio. Pulling it out of her back pocket, she was dismayed to find that it appeared to be dead. "The basement," she groaned. "It won't work down here."

Maria gave a half sob and Stephanie put an arm around her, trying to lend some warmth back into her shivering body. She checked the makeshift bandage as best she could by flashlight, pleased to see that the blood had not begun to seep through the cloth.

She felt Maria's terrified gaze on her. "Bandage is holding," she said with forced optimism. "Now let's find a way out of here."

Leaving Maria leaning against the wall to catch her breath, Stephanie explored the basement.

It was a small rectangular space, with cement walls. A series of pipes ran along the ceiling, and the floor was damp. Water dripped from cracks in the rock ceiling, indicating there was some source of groundwater nearby. Stephanie realized that she was becoming more chilled with every moment. Pushing aside her growing fear, she held the light as high as she could, searching for an exit.

Maria screamed, and she scrambled to her. "Something crawled over my feet."

"Mice, I think." Stephanie wished she had another jacket to give Maria. She worried the girl would go into shock or start bleeding profusely if the bullet wound was deeper than Stephanie had realized. Certainly the cold and fear was not good for Maria or her baby. "We'll get out of here soon. Let me check around some more."

Maria gave a shaky nod, cradling the violin, and Stephanie resumed her search. Her heart leaped when she saw a metal door, tucked behind a stack of bricks. The handle didn't budge when she turned it. She did not know if it was rusted shut or locked, but no matter how hard she tried, she succeeded only in loosening flakes of paint from the surface of the steel.

"Stephanie," Maria whispered. "I heard something."

Stephanie's stomach lurched. "Mice?"

"I don't think so."

The muffled sound of a gunshot filtered down to them. Stephanie's eyes locked in terror on Maria's.

Maria's hand went to her mouth. "Tate?"

Stephanie fought down the panic. "No. No, I'm sure it's not Tate. Maybe Ricardo is shooting through the door."

"Then he'll be down here in a few minutes. What are we going to do?"

*Well, we're not going to give up,* she thought, gritting her teeth. She prowled the space again, once more throwing her weight against the door until her shoulder ached. It still refused to give even the tiniest bit.

"Look for something we can use as a weapon." She had

Tate's knife in her pocket, but she did not want to have to get close enough to use it unless it was a last resort. Stephanie poked around the piles of debris until she came up with a section of a metal pole. It was not sharp, but it would do as a club since nothing better was at hand.

Stephanie pulled Maria behind the pile of bricks. It was a scant four feet high, but it was the only shelter available. Maria's lips were trembling as Stephanie tucked her behind the brick screen.

"Stay there. I'm going to stand at the bottom of the stairs, in the shadows. I'll trip him up or knock him out if I'm able to. Be ready to get up the stairs as fast as you can, okay?"

Maria shook her head. "I can't. I'm scared. I'm too scared."

Stephanie put her hands on Maria's shoulders to quell the mounting hysteria she heard in the girl's voice. "You can do it. You're tough, like your brother."

She didn't answer, so Stephanie bent her head to look Maria right in the eye. "Just get up the ladder and run. Find a place to hide."

Maria half sobbed. "Stephanie, what will happen to you?"

Stephanie forced a smile. "I'm tough, too, like *my* brothers. I'll meet you when I can."

"But what should I do with the violin?"

"Get it to Luca if you can. What's most important is that you make it out alive."

Maria caught Stephanie's hand before she moved away. "I'm really sorry. I'm so stupid. Forgive me."

"Forget it, Maria. You're forgiven as far as I'm concerned." Stephanie was comforted to know that she really meant it. It was a sweet feeling to truly forgive. She thought about Tate.

*Because every day I ask God to help me keep that bottle closed...*

And she realized in that moment that she had never asked God to help her forgive Tate, because she'd never wanted to. Being angry at him, resurrecting the past every time she thought of him, allowed her to keep from being hurt again.

Allowed her to hide from the pain, like he had hidden, buried deep in drugs.

A crash from above made them both jerk. Grasping her makeshift weapon, she gave Maria one final squeeze before she scurried to the stairwell. She paused to tuck the flashlight on top of a box and turned it on, the beam illuminating only the last few steps before she hid herself in the shadows at the foot of the staircase.

The creak of the trapdoor swinging open was followed by the thump of the cover being tossed aside. Stephanie fought to keep her breathing quiet.

Maybe the person coming down the stairs was Tate.

She hung on to the thought. He'd caught up with Eugene, and he was back looking for them.

But he would have called out, wouldn't he?

Maybe not, if he'd heard the shots.

Her palm grew sweaty where she gripped the iron bar. A squeal from the stairs indicated someone was on their way down.

One step, then another. Then a pause. Then a few more steps.

Stephanie kept count in her mind. Fifteen steps, and the person coming down had made it through seven. Five more steps, and they'd know if it was Tate...she swallowed hard.

Or Ricardo.

Her courage faltered for a moment, and she wondered if she would have the strength to overcome the man who'd shot Maria. If she didn't, Maria would have no chance, and neither would her baby.

Gripping the bar tighter, she waited for the footsteps to come closer.

A shadow crept into the glow of the flashlight. Stephanie's

heart pounded so hard she thought the person approaching must be able to hear it. Willing her knees to stop shaking, she watched as the shadow descended.

Her heart thudded to a stop. The shoes coming down the ladder were not Tate's.

She raised the bar.

It was wrenched from her hand so abruptly, she staggered back.

The figure stepped down into the light and tossed the bar into a far corner with a deafening clang.

"I've missed you, Stephanie," Joshua Bittman said.

# NINETEEN

Tate opened his eyes. When the blurriness subsided, he remembered why he was lying underneath a pile of broken crates. Ricardo.

Jerking fully to his senses, he kicked as hard as he could, knocking enough wood aside for him to scramble free. He was not sure how much time had passed as he ran to the room where he'd left Stephanie. The door was pocked with bullet holes and smashed open with such violence that the jamb had splintered.

Fear twisting his gut, he pushed inside, not sure what he might find.

The room was empty. A flicker of movement from outside the broken window caught his attention. He made it to the broken glass in time to watch Ricardo vanish into the tree line in the direction he thought he'd heard a helicopter earlier.

*He's checking it out.*

If Tate was right and Sartori had returned via helicopter, she'd have a chance to arrest him. Sartori was tough and savvy, a good match for Ricardo.

He returned his attention to the empty room. Droplets of something dark stained the corner floor. Blood. He swallowed the panic and searched farther, finding his way to the open trapdoor in moments. Some sort of basement.

His mind screamed at him. *Stephanie, get to Stephanie.* Throwing caution aside, he plunged down the ladder into the darkness, emerging at the bottom.

Stephanie stood there, seemingly unharmed, staring at him as deep gratitude filled every fiber of his body. He started forward, stopping abruptly as Joshua Bittman drew into the circle of light.

"What...?" The pieces fell into place. The chopper had not been Sartori's.

Bittman waved a small handgun in Tate's direction. "Ah, the oaf." He handed Stephanie a pair of plastic restraints. "Put them on him, please."

Stephanie's lips were pressed tightly together as she walked forward, circling his wrists with her fingers. Fear and anger shone in her eyes. She was trying to tell him something, but Bittman shifted so he could see her face. "Now."

He nodded to reassure her. *Buy time,* he wanted to say. *We'll get out of this somehow.*

Her touch was ice cold as she slipped the restraints around his wrists.

"Tightly," Bittman advised.

Stephanie complied. "You don't need to do this," she said. "We will get your violin."

"I know, but things were dreary back in San Francisco. Your father is a crotchety old man, trying to escape at every opportunity. He's quite wearing out my staff. I knew you were here in Lunkville."

"Did your spies fill you in?" Stephanie spat.

"When you worked for me, I had a device placed in your phone that activates the GPS and pings your location back to me." He laughed. "It also triggers the camera in your phone. I've gotten plenty of interesting snapshots of your life—everything from picnics to pie." His eyes swept over Stephanie.

Rage boiled up inside Tate. Bittman was more than a

crook; he was a deranged stalker, obsessed with Stephanie. "You're sick," he barked.

Bittman trained the gun on him. "And you are nothing. Poor, uneducated, powerless. You should have died in that crash instead of your father."

Tate jerked. "So you've been keeping tabs on me, too?"

"Only to make sure you were removed from Stephanie's life."

Tate opened his mouth to press further, but Bittman cut him off. "Where is she? Maria?"

Stephanie shrugged. "I don't know."

He smiled, teeth glinting in the lantern light. "Such a bad liar. There was blood in the outer room, and you're not injured. Either you managed to wound the person who shot up the door and window, or she's in here." He flicked on a small but powerful light and beamed it around the space.

"Maria, why don't you come out from behind those bricks? It's filthy back there."

Tate's mouth fell open as Maria emerged, violin in hand. His eyes were drawn immediately to the makeshift bandage around her waist.

"Are you hurt?"

She gave him a small smile. "Only a little. Ricardo shot through the window."

Bittman's eyebrows raised. "Ricardo? The man who worked at my father's shop?"

Tate watched Bittman as he mentally filled in the rest. *And the man who set the fire that killed my brother.*

"He's out there right now, checking out your helicopter," Tate said. "He was on his way to find Stephanie when he heard your approach. He might have shot you if you'd arrived a few minutes sooner. Pretty lethal for a pool guy."

"What are you blabbering about?"

Tate gave him a slow smile. "Oh, you didn't know that

Ricardo was working at your estate trying to ferret out information about the Guarneri? You have state-of-the-art security systems, and you didn't even know the enemy was right there on your property?"

Bittman's face was incredulous for a split second before the mask settled back into place. "Immaterial."

"You probably never even bothered to meet the pool guy. It must have been beneath you to rub elbows with the common folk. Feel stupid now, don't you, Bittman?"

Bittman's lip twitched. "He knew the Guarneri had resurfaced. He presumed the fastest way to find it was to let me do the work."

"Probably beats cleaning pools."

Bittman took a step toward him, and Tate figured he was in for a fist to the face. Stephanie tensed by him, but instead Bittman handed Stephanie another pair of restraints. "You may bind her, too."

Stephanie complied, leaving the bands loose around Maria's wrists until Bittman forced her to tighten them. While she did so, Bittman prowled the space, keeping the three in his peripheral vision.

With a catlike movement, he snatched up the violin. His eyes glittered, mouth curved into a smile. When he spoke, it was almost a whisper. "The Guarneri. Finally."

He gestured for them all to sit on the steps while he balanced the case on top of an overturned pallet. With trembling hands he opened it, his gaze roving over the interior like a hungry lion sizing up its prey.

He removed the violin and brought it closer to the lantern, which picked up the gleam of the rose-colored wood. Suddenly he jerked the violin from its case.

The three prisoners watched in astonishment as he brought the violin down full force on the pile of bricks, smashing it to bits.

\* \* \*

Stephanie cried out as pieces of the ruined instrument scattered over the space. "What are you doing?"

Bittman regarded the debris strewn across the floor. Then he turned to Maria. "It's a fake." He moved closer, and Tate stood in front of the two women.

"She didn't know that," Tate said.

Bittman raised the gun. "I don't care about you or your sister. I would be happy to kill both of you." He stared at Maria. "Where is my violin? Tell me, unless you would like me to shoot your brother, one limb at a time."

"No!" Maria cried.

"Don't tell him anything," Tate hissed.

Stephanie desperately tried to think of a way to help. Her hands were free, but she did not dare make any moves with Bittman's gun leveled at Tate.

Bittman's tone was flat. "You know I mean it, Maria, don't you? I am not a sentimental man. I will start with his crippled leg, and then the other. Then one arm…"

"Eugene has it," Maria yelped. "He must have given me the fake. He ran out with his backpack. He's here somewhere, close by, but he's not a troublemaker. Please don't hurt him."

Bittman shook off her comment. "That's better. We're going to find my violin and this tramp who took it. Back up the stairs. Now."

Stephanie went up the ladder after Maria, who moved slowly. She wondered how much blood Maria had lost from Ricardo's shot.

As they made their way out of the warehouse, she scanned the tree line. Ricardo would have discovered by now that the helicopter was Bittman's. In another few minutes, he would return to finish what he'd started. Stephanie saw Tate chafing against the restraints, which did nothing but cause them to cut into his wrists.

They left the building. Bittman surveyed the area. "Where would he hide?"

Maria shrugged. "Probably in one of the abandoned buildings along the road. We'll have to search."

Bittman stared at Tate. "Or maybe there's a faster way. Eugene!" he shouted. "You're here somewhere. I know you have my father's violin. I want it back. Come give it to me, and we'll let the whole matter drop."

The silence was broken only by the sound of an animal scavenging through the bushes.

"He's not here," Stephanie said.

"Eugene," Bittman said louder. "I'm sure you're a reasonable man. You don't want to be responsible for a murder, do you?"

Stephanie's blood went cold. Murder?

Bittman shoved Maria forward.

Tate charged, headfirst like a bull, but Bittman cuffed him on the head with the gun. He crashed to the ground, and Stephanie ran to him. By the time she'd helped him to his feet again, Bittman had the gun pressed to Maria's temple.

"This girl, she says she's a friend of yours, Eugene. Why don't you come out so we can talk? If you don't, I'll have to shoot her. She's pregnant, you know, so it would be two birds with one shot, so to speak."

Tate jerked, his eyes shifting from Maria to Stephanie.

She could see the question there. Pregnant? Stephanie nodded slowly, and Tate's face crumpled as he realized the truth.

It was as though she could see all the regret and shame unroll across his face like the subtitles in a movie. She'd told Bittman about the pregnancy, and he'd rejected her. Tate had failed his sister, removed himself from her life while he fought his own addiction. Now she was pregnant, with a gun to her head.

Bittman's attention was fixed on the entrance to the tunnel.

Stephanie remembered the knife in her pocket and the radio clipped to her belt. She sidled up a few inches closer, and Tate understood her intent. He quickly pulled the knife from her back pocket and hid it between his hands. She was trying to figure out how to access the radio without attracting attention when a voice floated out of the mine tunnel.

"She's my friend. Don't hurt her," a thin voice wailed.

Bittman smiled. "Of course I won't. Come out, Eugene. We have plenty to talk about."

"No."

Bittman shifted slightly, his tone soothing as if he spoke to a child. "Then I'll have to shoot her. That would be sad, wouldn't it, Eugene? She's so pretty. It would be your fault, too."

Stephanie wanted to call out to the terrified man, to tell him about the monster named Bittman, but she was too scared of the gun pressing into the side of Maria's head.

The board across the cave entrance trembled. "Don't hurt her. You can come in."

Bittman's eyebrow raised. "How do I know you have the violin?"

There was a long pause, and then the sound of music, light and delicate as windblown petals, danced through the air.

Stephanie had never heard any sound more beautiful.

The reaction in Bittman was shocking. He tensed, mouth slightly open, the veins on his neck standing out.

"You learned that song from my father. He played it all the time." Bittman's hand tightened around the gun.

She saw Tate edging closer, and she did the same.

The music kept on, Bittman's voice rising over the sweet melody. "You learned that from my father, and then you stole his instrument. How dare you? He let you live in our shop, eat from our table, and you stole from him." A drop of spittle flew from Bittman's mouth. "Stop playing, stop immediately."

The song died away.

Bittman took a deep breath, and his tone was calmer when he spoke. "I will kill her if you don't come out."

"You'll kill me if I do," Eugene said, voice hoarse.

Bittman wiped a hand over his mouth. "We're running out of time. There's another man here, the one who set the fire. It is a matter of time before he arrives to kill you. I merely want the violin. Give it to me, and I will let you go."

"And Maria?"

Bittman looked at Maria as if he'd forgotten about her. "Yes."

A soft thud indicated Eugene was kicking at the boards from the inside. One finally fell away, revealing a dark hole.

"You can come in," Eugene said. "If you promise not to kill her."

Bittman smiled, and the chill in his expression took Stephanie's breath away.

*No, Eugene. He'll kill you. He'll kill us all.*

But no words would come.

Bittman shoved Maria ahead of him, then gestured with the gun for Stephanie and Tate to follow her. In his panicked state, if Eugene had a weapon, he would use it on one of them first, she thought grimly.

With hands thrust before her, she stepped into the perfect darkness.

# TWENTY

Tate kept the knife pressed between his palms, waiting for the chance to cut off his restraints. For all his intellectual prowess, Bittman had made a mistake by having Stephanie cuff his hands in front instead of behind. All he had to do was work the knife blade back and forth. The mine was dark enough to allow him cover. The blade was positioned point up, toward his wrists. As he wriggled it into place, the blade cut into his palms. Gritting his teeth, he began to saw away at the plastic.

The interior of the shaft was a small space, no more than eight feet across, and he had to duck his head to keep from hitting it on the ceiling.

"No games, Eugene," Bittman said. "Turn on a light."

Instead the sound of the violin filled the tiny cavern, echoing along the low beams that supported the ceiling. It was the same haunting melody.

"Stop it," Bittman's voice thundered. "Stop playing my father's song."

"He meant for me to play it," Eugene said over the music. "He meant for me to have the Guarneri."

Tate could hear Bittman's teeth snap together.

"He meant it for his son, for my brother, Peter, you cretin." The music stopped abruptly. "Peter."

There was an odd questioning tone in Eugene's word. "Peter," he repeated. "Peter Bittman. Have you seen him?"

Bittman grunted. "He's dead. Ricardo burned down the shop and killed him."

"That's sad," Eugene said, beginning to play again.

"Stop!" Bittman roared.

The music kept going, faster now.

Tate's fingers kept time as he sliced away at the restraints.

Bittman yelled and Eugene continued to play, the song growing wilder with each measure.

Bittman fired off a shot that drilled itself into the ceiling, hurting Tate's ears. The impact of the bullet made a tiny puff of sparks.

Eugene broke off playing.

"Now," Bittman said quietly as a lighter flared to life in his hand, illuminating the gun still pointed at Maria. "There is a lantern there, hanging on the wall. Light it."

Tate felt the plastic beginning to give.

Eugene lifted a trembling hand to the lantern and lit it. He stood there with the violin cradled in his arm, his beard covered by dust.

Bittman moved forward into the lantern light. "Give me the violin."

"*Vater* meant me to have it. He would not have wanted it to burn. I ran. I ran to keep it safe." His voice dropped to a whisper, hands stroking the violin. "Safe."

Bittman stared at Eugene. *"Vater?"* He moved closer to Eugene, who cowered against the wall, then staggered a step back as if he'd been struck. Tate was dismayed to see he did not lower the weapon. "Peter."

"Peter," Eugene repeated thoughtfully.

"You are my brother, Peter," Bittman whispered. "But you died in the fire."

Stephanie spoke quickly as the truth sizzled through her.

"The body was badly burned. It was twenty years ago. It was probably the homeless man your father took in. Peter was the one who took the violin. Peter was the one you saw that night running away."

Bittman's glance flicked from Stephanie back to Eugene.

Tate's wrists finally came clear of the restraints. He lunged at Bittman, knocking the gun from his hand, which skittered away into the darkness. Eugene let out a cry and shrank back.

Tate tumbled to the floor, fighting for a grip on Bittman, who was trying to dig his fingers into Tate's throat. They crashed into the stone walls, thrashing as Tate grappled to loosen Bittman's choke hold.

Tate was fueled by a strength he didn't know he had. This time he would not fail his sister, and Stephanie would be free of Joshua Bittman forever. Inch by inch, he managed to force Bittman's hands away from his throat, maneuvering him onto his stomach. Tate's knee was across his shoulder blades.

He sat panting, hands bloody and leg twitching with pain.

"I will have my violin," Bittman said, his voice filled with hatred. "And my brother will come home."

Eugene looked confused. "Home?"

"Oh, I don't think so," came a voice from the mouth of the cavern. Tate's heart dropped like a stone as Ricardo stepped into the space, a gun gripped in his hand. "So I'm not responsible for killing your brother after all," he said.

"But you killed the homeless guy and Devlin," Tate panted. "You're still a murderer."

Ricardo shrugged. "It's like potato chips. Hard to have just one." He laughed. "I appreciate you doing the legwork for me, boy. Here is my violin, and all the people I need to kill in one spot."

Tate started to rise.

"Slowly," Ricardo warned. "I think maybe we'll take this party outside. Ladies first."

Tate got off Bittman, who climbed to his feet. They paraded out of the mine shaft into the predawn.

Ricardo took the violin from Eugene's hand. Bittman twitched as he watched Ricardo tuck the instrument under his arm.

"You know, I've got the perfect way to tidy up this mess." He led them down a dusty section of road to the old jail they'd searched earlier. "Everyone inside."

"My pilot will radio for help if I'm not back soon," Bittman said.

Ricardo shook his head. "He would if he was still conscious."

Tate's stomach lurched. "Let the women go. You don't need to hurt them."

He smiled. "Right. I'm sure they wouldn't tell anyone about me." He guided them inside. "No, I like the irony of this method. This way, Peter really will die in a fire, just like he supposedly did twenty years ago, only he'll have company. I just need to get the gas can from that ridiculous Volkswagen. It's hidden nearby. I won't keep you waiting long."

Tate tried desperately to find a way to fight back, but anything he might have tried would result in the death of one of their group. He followed the women into the jail, along with Eugene. Ricardo pushed Bittman inside last.

He whirled to face Ricardo, his body tense like a cat ready to spring. "I'll find you. No matter where you go, I'll find you."

"No," Ricardo said, leaning in as though he was divulging a secret. "You'll die."

Bittman's hands curved into claws. "I have people who will track you down, and you won't even realize they're onto you."

"Only if they take orders from a dead guy," Ricardo said with a laugh.

Bittman was trembling with rage. "A small puncture in your brake line, and you'll be gone."

Tate started. The brake line?

*You should have died in that crash, instead of your father.*

Tate's pulse thundered. "You tried to have me killed, didn't you? By tampering with the brakes of my truck."

Bittman's hatred was palpable. "And you managed to make a mess of that, too, and your father died instead."

Somewhere in the back of his mind, he heard Maria gasp.

"Why...?" Stephanie whispered.

Bittman turned to her. "He's a loser. A nobody, and he couldn't give you anything close to what you deserved."

Before Tate realized it, his hands were clutching Bittman's collar.

Ricardo laughed again. "I'm sorry to miss this, but I've got a plane to catch and a violin to sell. Adios."

The sound of the door swinging closed roused Tate from his red-hot rage. He threw himself at it, fists making contact in time to feel the heavy bolt slide shut from the outside.

Stephanie could hardly absorb what she'd just heard. Bittman had tried to murder Tate and instead killed Mr. Fuego. She hadn't realized until that moment Bittman's level of depravity, his need to possess her. The list of tragedies that stemmed from Bittman's dark obsession was growing: Victor, her father, Mr. Fuego, Devlin and now more people awaited death in a space that would become an inferno if Ricardo had his way. For a moment she teetered on the edge of despair.

*Lord, I'm still here. You made me strong for a reason. Help me now.*

She and Tate immediately began to examine the walls as best they could in the darkness, the only light coming from cracks in the roof, testing for any weaknesses. Fifteen frantic minutes passed until there was a sound of crumpling paper and the acrid smell of gasoline.

Eugene's voice was a whisper. "Fire. He's going to burn it down." He began to cry.

Maria put her arm around Eugene. "It's going to be okay. I loved the song you played on the violin. Can you tell me about it?"

Stephanie shot her a grateful look. Maria was going to be a good mother, if they could get her out alive. She could just see Tate's staunch profile. He would not stop trying until they were free or dead. He was one of the few people who could match her determination.

All this time she'd refused to forgive him for his failures, deep down holding on to lingering resentment. Now it seemed that the situation had flipped. Her dealings with Bittman had cost him his father, ruined his sister. He would not be able to forgive that, and she did not blame him.

Remembering the radio in her pocket, she turned it on, only to receive buzzing static. She spoke into it anyway, explaining the situation in as few words as she could manage. Then she handed it to Maria. "Keep talking on it. Maybe someone will hear."

Bittman pulled out his cell phone. He got no signal, which was not a surprise. It wouldn't matter anyway. The flicker of flames showed under the gap in the door, and acrid smoke poured in.

Stephanie looked for something to stuff under the crack. Maria handed her the jacket that had been wrapped around her waist. "The bleeding has stopped. Use this."

Cramming the fabric in the gap slowed the smoke to a trickle, but it would not hold for long, Stephanie knew. She joined Tate, hands pressing over the rough bricks, looking for the smallest weakness in the old walls.

Bittman stood defiantly in the center of the space, occasionally looking at his brother, who was rocking back and forth next to Maria. The man who had wreaked havoc on so many lives was now powerless, like a snake with his fangs removed. Stephanie continued on, her fingers raw from the rough walls.

The crackle of flames grew louder as the fire traveled up the side of the old jail and started to gain a foothold on the roof.

"Fire, fire," Eugene moaned as Maria tried to comfort him.

The radio crackled, and a voice came through. "Repeat."

Stephanie felt a surge of hope. If Sartori was close…

There was another burst of static, and the voice died away. Maria began her message all over again, but there was no further acknowledgment. Stephanie turned away from Maria rather than see the hope die in her eyes.

Tate grunted, dropping to his knees in the far corner. She went to him, thinking he'd been injured.

"One loose," he said, pushing at a silvered brick with his palms. Slowly, the block began to move under the steady pressure. He got to his feet and began to kick at it. Stephanie could only imagine the pain it caused his damaged leg. When he paused to recover for a moment, Stephanie took his place, throwing kick after kick against the weakened spot.

Tate pulled her aside. "The smoke is thicker." He jerked a thumb at the others.

Stephanie needed no further instructions. She turned to Maria and Eugene. "Lay down on the floor where the air is cleaner." She spoke gently to Eugene. "May I have your shirt, Eugene? I promise I'll buy you another when we get out of here."

He nodded and gave her his outer flannel shirt, leaving him in a stained white T-shirt. She tore off the two sleeves and handed one to them. "Cover your nose and mouth. Breath through the cloth."

She turned with the body of the shirt in her hands and held it to Bittman. "You can use this," she forced herself to say.

"Stephanie, if only you had seen reason when we first met." He touched her hand, and she jerked it away.

"If I had been reasonable then, I never would have gone to work for you."

He laughed. "I have always admired your fire. That drive is what attracts me to you, and your refusal only increases that attraction."

"Why don't you try to comfort your brother?" She could not stand to hear one more word from Joshua Bittman. "Lie down if you want to live." She turned back to Tate just as he aimed a vicious kick at the loosened brick. It slid free, plopping into the dust outside the jail and letting in a stream of smoky light, the weak rays of early dawn.

He beamed a triumphant smile at her that made her breath catch.

"We just need to make an opening big enough to crawl through." He began kicking at the bricks again, but she could see that his leg was weakening.

She edged in front. "We'll take turns. This round is mine."

Tate was panting too hard to answer, but he nodded and she went to work, blasting at the weakening spot as hard as she could, each impact jarring her to the bone.

A second brick gave a fraction of a centimeter, and it sent her energy into overdrive. She kicked like a wild horse until the second brick gave way, bringing a third with it.

Tate took over while she caught her breath. The air was now thick with smoke, curling upward to the rafters above. Pops and crackles filled the air. She realized that the outside roof had caught, and the fire was eating away at the beams.

In spite of his extreme effort, Tate only managed to loosen the next brick.

"Let me try now," she said.

He barred her with his arm. "No." His jaw gritted, and he struck out with renewed effort. The air had grown hotter with each passing moment, and sweat poured down both their faces. She shot a look at Maria and Eugene, who lay on their stomachs on the floor.

She was just about to insist that Tate give her another turn when an ominous crack sounded above them. Jerking her head, she was horrified to see a jagged piece of burning wood from the ceiling give way. It tumbled through the air, landing right next to Eugene.

He leaped up with a cry, waving his arms around.

"Stop!" Stephanie yelled. "Please, Eugene, stop!"

Her words had no effect as he whirled madly, as the white fabric of his T-shirt caught fire.

Tate jerked toward the sharp cry of pain. Through the smoke he could make out Eugene flapping his burning sleeve, fanning the flames with his panic.

Bittman followed him helplessly. "Peter, listen to me, listen to me!" he shouted louder and louder until he was hollering, but his brother was so caught up in the fear he did not or could not hear him.

Tate moved as quickly as he could, his leg nearly folding underneath him. He pushed by Bittman and knocked Eugene to the floor, hearing the air forced from Eugene's lungs by the impact.

When they hit the floor, Tate began rolling Eugene back and forth. Mercifully the panic seemed to be knocked out of Eugene along with the impact, and he lay relatively passively while Tate smothered the flames. When he was satisfied the fabric was no longer burning, he got up and helped Eugene to a sitting position. Maria came closer, speaking soothingly.

Bittman pushed them both aside. "Get away. He's my brother. I will take care of him."

Bittman sat carefully on the floor, knees folded underneath him, and put a tentative hand on Eugene's back. "When we get out of here, things will change, Peter. You will come back to live with me, where you belong. You will have anything you want."

Eugene's lips were tight with the pain from his burned arm. "I want my violin," he sobbed. "My violin."

Bittman's eyes glittered, hard and cold. "You will have it. I promise."

Tate did not have time to puzzle over Bittman's unfounded confidence. He'd managed to knock only four bricks loose, and he'd need to push out twice that many to make the hole large enough for them to crawl through. The jail was now alive with smoke and the ominous hiss and crack of the fire on the roof. He ducked down to avoid breathing in the black smoke and returned to the corner. Stephanie joined him, and they resumed their tag team effort. She was exhausted, he could tell by the droop of her head, but she worked as hard as humanly possible to shove out a brick, which took another one with it.

She grinned and gave him a double thumbs-up.

Suddenly the task seemed doable, fueled by the light in her eyes and the triumphant smile on her face. It had always been that way, he thought. With Stephanie in his life, he had the courage and optimism that eluded him in the dark days they'd been apart.

But not completely, he realized as he kicked out at the bricks. In the horrifying aftermath of his father's death, he'd summoned strength to beat back the addiction that clung to him like a shadow.

It was God-given strength; it could be nothing else. He'd been blessed with an extraordinary woman to love, and even in the darkest moments of despair he had the memory of that love to remind him he had been worth something—worth loving, worth grieving for, as he knew Stephanie had done.

His shame at his past began to fall away, like the flakes of mortar that drifted through the smoky air. It was true, he had been neither the man nor the brother he should have been, but he could push by that, kick away at the wall of sin and glimpse the brilliant future that lay on the other side.

He felt a surge of energy ripple through his body, and he hammered his boot against the wall, unaware that Eugene, Bittman and Maria had joined them until Maria cried out as brick number seven fell away.

Stephanie put her hand on Tate's shoulder, and he clasped it there for a moment, drawing new strength from her touch.

"I'll finish," Stephanie said. "You need to rest."

He looked at her, so tired, her face streaked with soot and more beautiful to him than raindrops on roses. This was a woman who taught him that he was worthy of loving. "No, Steph," he said quietly. "I'm going to finish this."

With his leg screaming in pain, he began anew until finally, with torturous slowness, another brick fell and two more besides. The hole would be big enough, barely.

Bittman made for it, pulling his brother behind, but Tate blocked them. "The women go first."

Bittman's lip curled as he considered. For a moment, Tate thought he would need to physically restrain Bittman and his brother, but suddenly he stepped back. "As you wish," he said, something in his tone causing alarm bells to jingle in the back of Tate's mind.

As Maria squeezed through, a burning beam fell through into the center of the space with a whoosh that catapulted burning embers in a whirlwind around them.

"Go now!" Tate shouted over the rising sound of burning wood. He grabbed Stephanie's shoulders and shoved her into the hole. He watched in relief as she wriggled through.

It took coaxing from the women outside and the men inside to convince Eugene to shimmy through, scraping his burned shoulder as he did so.

Maria crooned to him the whole time, soft words of comfort, until he was gone.

Then Tate was alone with Bittman, flames licking the walls around them.

"Last men standing," Bittman said. "Ironic."

"Get going." A spurt of flame from above their heads distracted him just long enough. Bittman pulled a knife from his coat pocket and plunged it into Tate's side.

The shock was so intense that he stood there for a moment, just long enough to see the triumph on Bittman's face.

"Last man standing," he purred.

Tate pulled the knife out and fell forward, watching Bittman vanish through the broken wall of bricks.

# TWENTY-ONE

Stephanie helped Maria try to soothe Eugene, but all the while she eyed the gap. Bittman emerged, as calm as if he'd just left a board meeting. The moments ticked by, and there was no sign of Tate. Flames were now dancing madly across the roof as she ran back to the hole, Maria right behind her.

"Tate," she yelled into the smoking jail. "Where are you?"

There was no answer, and she pushed her head and shoulders back in the gap. "Tate." Her heart convulsed as she saw him there, lying on the floor, blood staining his shirt.

"Get out," he said in a voice so soft, she almost didn't hear it above the flames.

She willed her voice to stay steady. "I'm coming in to get you."

"No," he said louder. "You need to get out. Keep Maria safe, and call the cops. The ceiling's going to go. Steph, I…"

Tate's words were drowned out by a massive boom. She felt Maria yank on her shoulder, and she was drawn backward as the ceiling collapsed, forcing the brick wall to buckle.

"Tate!" she screamed. Even before the ground stopped rumbling, she was scrambling back toward him. Through a cloud of choking debris, she could just make out that the bricks had compacted, covering over the hard-won hole. Now the building was an impenetrable six-foot-wall of brick, crowned by a burning roof. She ran around it, desperately looking for a gap, a small opening that would allow her to get in, but she found nothing.

Maria pressed her hands to her mouth, her eyes round with horror. "Oh, Steph," she whispered.

Stephanie's body went cold even as her brain searched for options.

The fight wasn't over, it couldn't be. An idea shot through her brain.

She grabbed Maria's wrists. "Use the radio and call the police."

"What are you going to do?" she heard Maria call as she sprinted madly down the road.

What was she doing? The most insane thing she could think of, but it was the only way that might save Tate. She prayed as she tore along, stumbling and sliding on loose gravel, slapping branches out of her way. *Let him hold on, Lord.*

She'd found her share of priceless items, paintings and coins, pottery and gems, but never had she felt the excruciating urgency that coursed through her body. Inside that burning jail, buried under filth and ashes, was the greatest treasure she'd been blessed to possess, damaged though it was.

Nothing from the past mattered anymore. Not one moment of it.

Panting, sweat running down her face, she made it to the car, snatching the keys from her pocket with trembling hands.

In a moment, she'd gunned the engine and turned the vehicle back up the slope, bouncing over ruts, rocks pinging against the undercarriage.

*Hold on, Tate. Hold on.* Her mind screamed as she pushed the car faster, the tires spinning along the trail. Past the ruined houses and the tower. She could see the black smoke rising in a roiling mass just over the next hill.

The rear tire exploded, and the car skidded to one side. Stephanie fought to keep control. Now wobbling madly, the vehicle was a hundred yards from the jail. She shot past it and slammed on the brakes, the rear end skidding until the car was once again facing the jail.

It was almost concealed under a blanket of smoke, orange flames darting through gaps in the broken bricks. She aimed the car directly at the far side of the jail, farthest away from the spot she knew Tate had fallen.

With a last prayer, body prickled in goose bumps, she pressed the gas pedal to the floor. The car leaped forward, thunking on the ruined tire. Faster and faster it accelerated, until the scenery flew by in a blur.

The gap closed quickly—fifteen feet, then twelve, six, four, three.

Stephanie closed her eyes just before the car crashed into the wall of bricks.

Tate watched the smoke billow in graceful arcs around him. It would kill him before the flames, he knew. At least the others had made it out. Stephanie would take care of Maria, and keep her safe from Bittman.

It was the one thing that pricked at his mind. Bittman had made it out unscathed. He would no doubt spend the rest of his life tracking down Ricardo, and Tate knew he would probably win in the end. He'd have his violin and his vengeance.

But he wouldn't have Stephanie. He would not possess the one thing he craved the most.

He pictured her smile again, giving him the double thumbs-up, eyes dancing with triumph.

A troubling fact intruded. Bittman still had Stephanie's father, and as long as he did, he'd have his hooks into her.

Pain rippled through his leg and the wound in his side. A fit of coughing escalated the agony, and he closed his eyes against it. Sparks rained down on him, and he became aware of an out-of-place sound—the sound of an approaching engine.

Maybe it was Sartori.

He felt a surge of satisfaction. She had probably missed the chance to capture Bittman, but knowing help was there for Stephanie and Maria eased his mind. The sound grew louder, but his coughing drowned it out.

A split second later, there was a grinding crash and the far wall of the jail exploded, sending bricks flying like cement missiles through the air. He covered his head, unable to fathom a reason for the implosion until he looked up again. There was the wrecked rental car, the front end jacked up on a pile of debris. The door opened, and Stephanie spilled out.

He was imagining it, the carbon monoxide confusing his mind.

She scrambled over the bricks, heedless of the smoke, and knelt next to him.

"Tate?" she whispered, face tight with fear.

"Steph, did you just drive the car through the wall?"

She nodded as she hooked her hands under his arms to help him rise. "You always said if there wasn't a door, I'd make a window."

In spite of the pain in his side, he laughed.

They emerged in the sunlight to see Sartori arrive with Luca in the front seat. Sartori took one look at them and grabbed the first-aid kit. Luca helped Stephanie ease Tate on a rock while Sartori pressed a section of gauze to the wound in his side as Stephanie told them the details.

"It's only a scratch," Tate said.

"More like a dent," Sartori countered, "but I think you'll live. Paramedics are on their way."

Luca wrapped Stephanie in his arms and kissed the top of her head as she told him about Bittman and Ricardo and Eugene's true identity.

Maria ran up and hugged her brother, tears streaming down her face.

"Tate, I was so scared," she sobbed. He rubbed a hand on her back.

"It's okay."

She drew back abruptly. "You're bleeding."

"Bittman decided to leave me with a final souvenir. He missed any vital organs, I think, because I'm still alive. He escaped with Eugene."

Sartori nodded, a look of satisfaction transforming her face. She jerked a thumb at the backseat of her police car. "Not exactly."

Stephanie jerked in amazement. Bittman sat in stony silence, staring out the window of Sartori's car. Bear stood outside the door, ears pricked and body on full alert.

"I told you Bear was effective," Sartori said. The dog twitched at his name but did not budge from his post near Bittman. "We saw him making his way back down to the main road, and Bear was obliging enough to catch him. We had plenty of grounds to arrest him because your father was quite happy to fill us in on his abduction by Mr. Bittman."

Stephanie gasped. "Dad? You found him?"

Luca beamed. "Tuney did, actually. He wasn't about to give up, just like he said. Dad's perfectly fine, except he's lost a few pounds and he's got a gash to the head. Tuney was trying to talk him out of storming here immediately to help."

Tears flowed down Stephanie's face, but she wiped them away and turned fearful eyes to Luca. "Victor?" she whispered.

"He's okay. He beat the infection, and he's fully conscious.

As soon as I saw him, I turned right around to come back here."

Stephanie felt her knees crumple under her, and both Tate and Luca helped her to sit on the rock next to Tate. Her nerves were firing so many emotions at once, she was not sure which to feel first. Victor and her father were okay. The joy threatened to overwhelm her.

Luca looked solemnly at Tate. "You saved my sister, and you almost died in the process. Thank you."

Tate nodded.

Luca hesitated. "I've misjudged you."

"I gave you good reason." Tate lifted his chin, his face bruised and battered. "I'm clean. I want you to know that. I've been clean for a year, and I'm going to stay that way."

Luca cocked his head. "I believe you mean that." Slowly he extended a hand. "Let's make a fresh start then."

Tate and Luca shook hands. Stephanie saw the look pass between them, a look of trust and respect. Her heart skipped a beat.

Luca chuckled. "You know, I can't believe we actually did it. We found the violin and Bittman's supposedly dead brother. Incredible."

Stephanie saw no sign of him. "Where is Eugene?"

"Sartori had another officer transport him to the hospital."

"What will happen to him?"

"We'll see that he gets the help he needs since big brother will be in jail," Sartori said. "Long list of complaints, abduction, your brother's accident, Devlin's death."

"And my father's murder," Tate cut in.

Sartori's eyebrows nearly vanished into her hairline. "I didn't know about that one. We'll have to get those details. I got word that they've stopped Ricardo Williams at the airport, so eventually Eugene, or Peter rather, may get his violin back."

An ambulance arrived, and the paramedics began to check over Maria and Tate. Luca used Sartori's satellite phone to call the hospital and fill in Victor and their father on the situation. Stephanie found herself drawn to the police car, to the rigid figure sitting in the back. She did not know why she wanted to see him—maybe to convince herself that he really was no longer a threat to herself and the people she loved.

Sartori saw her approach and called Bear away from the car.

Bittman turned to look at her, his gaze an odd mixture of regret and desire. "I could have given you anything you wanted."

*Sometimes what you want isn't what you need.* She needed a partner, a soul mate, a strong man who looked to God in the darkest of times. A man who drove a beat-up truck and matched her in both stubbornness and determination. Her throat thickened. A man who had nearly exchanged his life for hers. But too much had driven a wedge between them, including the man who sat there now, staring at her imperiously as though his hands were not in cuffs. Her eyes turned toward Tate.

"You made the wrong choice," Bittman said, following her gaze.

*Yes, I did.* Tate's eyes sought hers, and for a fleeting moment, she wondered if one more choice could change everything. Then he lowered his head and looked away.

She gave Bittman one final glance. "I don't belong to you. I never did, and I never will."

She returned to her brother, who was still talking on the phone. Maria sat nearby, a blood pressure cuff on her arm. She beamed a smile at Stephanie.

"The baby is okay. They heard the heartbeat."

Stephanie smiled. Maria's love would be enough for her unborn child. "I'm so glad, Maria."

Another paramedic worked on Tate and gave her a nod. "We'll transport him to the hospital."

"I don't need to go," Tate said, his chin set stubbornly. "It's just a scratch."

Stephanie folded her arms. "But you're going anyway because Baby Fuego is going to need his or her uncle around for a long time."

Tate grumbled and then cracked a smile. "Uncle Tate. Has a nice ring to it." He hesitated. "Are you okay? That was some crash."

She flushed at the way his eyes roved her face. "Perfectly fine."

Luca clicked off the phone with a grin. "When I told him how things worked out here, Victor let out such a whoop the nurse dropped her medicine tray. I believe his exact words were, 'we've got a wedding to plan.'"

Sartori called Luca over, and he clapped Tate on the back and gave Stephanie a kiss.

Stephanie couldn't help but smile. "A happy ending."

Tate was silent, staring off at the distant hills.

"Anyway, thank you, Tate." The words seemed woefully inadequate. "I didn't deserve your help." She felt the tears sting her eyes. "You put yourself on the line for my father, after Bittman took away yours."

He still kept his face turned away, and she knew that he thought it, too: *if you had only listened to me...believed in me...*

"I didn't do any of this for your father," he said quietly.

She looked at Maria, resting in the shelter of a tree while the paramedics finished their work. He'd done it for Maria, to make up for his failure with her. Family ties really were the strongest. He loved his sister, she loved her brothers, and Bittman, perhaps as much as he was capable of it, loved Peter.

Luca's laughter caught her attention. Soon she would be

home, back in San Francisco, working with her brothers again.

And Tate would be living his own life, as far away from her as two hearts could be.

She felt a stab of pain.

"I did it," Tate said, looking at her now, "for you."

Her stomach flipped as she looked into his clear gray eyes.

"I did it because I love you. In my mind, you are my perfect match."

She stared, not believing what was coming from his mouth. "What are you saying?"

"I've got an idea," he said, abruptly getting to his feet with a wince of pain.

"Sit down. You've been hurt."

"Nope. Gotta do this standing up."

Something in his face made her heart skip a beat. "Do what?"

"Your brother's finally going to have his happy ending with Brooke. Let's make it two."

"What do you mean?"

"A double wedding. Victor and Brooke…and you and me."

Stephanie's mouth fell open. "We can't."

"Why not?" Tate pulled her into the circle of his arms.

"We tried and things fell apart. I…I didn't want to forgive you."

"And I didn't want to forgive myself. But that's changed now." He traced his fingers over her face, keeping her gaze riveted to his.

"I brought Bittman into our lives, and your father…" Tears slipped down her cheeks.

He hugged her closer and traced the curve of her cheekbone with his lips. "We made mistakes. Both of us. I feel like I got a second chance to start over, and I want to spend the rest of my life celebrating that with you."

Her skin prickled as she leaned against him, his hand on the small of her back. "Tate, there's too much…"

"No," he whispered in her ear. "There's just enough. Just enough love to keep us together in this crazy life, to keep us strong for each other."

Just enough love? Did she have enough love and strength left to turn her back on their dark past? "Tate, I…"

She broke off, lost in a rush of emotion that sounded over her like the sweetest note of a haunting song. All she had to do was give the past to God and take hold of the future with which God had blessed them both.

"I love you, Tate," she whispered, turning her face to his.

"I've sure waited a long time to hear that," he said, his voice hoarse.

She was almost sure, as his mouth found hers, that she could hear an exquisite melody that was theirs alone.

\* \* \* \* \*

*Look for Dana Mentink's next*
TREASURE SEEKERS *novel,*
FINAL RESORT, *available in February*
*from Love Inspired Suspense.*

Dear Reader,

This week we watched a wonderful baby dedication at our church. The youth group led the little preschoolers in a song that brought down the house, so to speak. I know my eyes were certainly damp! We all cooed over the adorable children, God's precious treasures. It struck me that as we change and grow, like that innocent baby into adulthood, sometimes we lose our way and forget that we are treasures in God's eyes. Swept up in circumstances and world-weary, we drift far away from that understanding, don't we? The good news is, no matter how far we drift, no matter how broken we become, God will find us because we are His treasures, priceless in His eyes. *For the Son of Man came to seek and to save what was lost.* Luke 19:10.

Thank you for joining me in this second book in the Treasure Seekers series. The next book will focus on Luca Gage as he embarks on a wild hunt to find a "pearl of great price" inadvertently acquired by a missing man in the purchase of an abandoned storage unit. Dangerous times are ahead for the Gage family as this series wraps up.

I welcome comments from my readers. You can reach me via my webpage at www.danamentink.com, and my physical address is there also for those who prefer corresponding by mail.

Thank you sincerely for spending some precious time with me!

Fondly,

Dana Mentink

## Questions for Discussion

1. Stephanie Gage is thrown into a deadly situation because of bad decisions made earlier in her life. How do past mistakes intrude upon our present lives? What are some biblical examples of how to handle such situations?

2. Joshua Bittman is a man obsessed with having his own way. Have you had experience with people who share this trait? How do they deal with defeat?

3. The Treasure Seekers pursue a priceless violin made by Guarneri del Gesu. What other prizes do modern-day treasure hunters seek? Can you recall any treasures that have recently made the news?

4. Tate shut Stephanie and Maria out of his life when he succumbed to addiction. Was it right to keep them away from the situation? Why or why not?

5. Stephanie and Tate are very different, but also share some strong similarities. What character traits do they have in common? Are these helpful traits or hindrances?

6. How can we be mindful of our past failures, and still move forward to live the life God intends for us?

7. Do you think it's a good idea for Tate to continually carry around a reminder of his addiction? Why or why not?

8. Ex-cop Tuney makes an appearance in this story. What would be a happy ending for him? Do you suppose such an ending would be possible for a man of his character?

9. If you could embark on your own treasure hunt, what prize would you search for? Explain.

10. Tate will have to fight his addiction all his life, but he has chosen to look forward to his future. Is there an area of your life where you are making the same choice? What is the benefit to making that decision? The cost?

11. Stephanie's plan to free Tate from the burning jail is extreme. Would you have done the same? Why or why not?

12. Luca will take the lead in the final installment of the Treasure Seekers series. What treasure do you imagine he will be looking for? What roadblocks will he face on his way to finding a soul mate?

## COMING NEXT MONTH
### from Love Inspired® Suspense
AVAILABLE NOVEMBER 20, 2012

### BETRAYAL ON THE BORDER
**Jill Elizabeth Nelson**

As the only survivors of a massive ambush, former army communications specialist Maddie Jerrard and investigative journalist Chris Mason have a killer on their trail. To survive, now they'll have to trust each other.

### CHRISTMAS COUNTDOWN
*Lost, Inc.*
**Vicki Hinze**

Trapped in a serial killer's deadly game of cat and mouse, Maggie finds an ally in private investigator Dr. Ian Crane. Love could cost them everything....unless they can find their way to each other in time for Christmas.

### A PROMISE TO PROTECT
**Liz Johnson**

Navy SEAL Matt Waterstone promises to keep Ashley Sawyer and the residents of the women's shelter she runs safe. Once Ashley falls prey to a crime web, she must trust Matt to keep her alive.

### TREACHEROUS SKIES
**Elizabeth Goddard**

Abducted and stashed on a plane, Maya Carpenter's only hope is daredevil pilot Connor Jacobson. Connor has a few tricks that might keep them safe...if he's willing to put everything at risk, including his heart.

LISCNM1112

# REQUEST YOUR FREE BOOKS!

## 2 FREE RIVETING INSPIRATIONAL NOVELS
## PLUS 2 FREE MYSTERY GIFTS

*Love Inspired.*
## SUSPENSE

---

**YES!** Please send me 2 FREE Love Inspired® Suspense novels and my 2 FREE mystery gifts (gifts are worth about $10). After receiving them, if I don't wish to receive any more books, I can return the shipping statement marked "cancel". If I don't cancel, I will receive 4 brand-new novels every month and be billed just $4.49 per book in the U.S. or $4.99 per book in Canada. That's a saving of at least 22% off the cover price. It's quite a bargain! Shipping and handling is just 50¢ per book in the U.S. and 75¢ per book in Canada.* I understand that accepting the 2 free books and gifts places me under no obligation to buy anything. I can always return a shipment and cancel at any time. Even if I never buy another book, the two free books and gifts are mine to keep forever.

123/323 IDN FEHR

| | |
|---|---|
| Name | (PLEASE PRINT) |

| | |
|---|---|
| Address | Apt. # |

| | | |
|---|---|---|
| City | State/Prov. | Zip/Postal Code |

Signature (if under 18, a parent or guardian must sign)

Mail to the **Reader Service:**
**IN U.S.A.:** P.O. Box 1867, Buffalo, NY  14240-1867
**IN CANADA:** P.O. Box 609, Fort Erie, Ontario  L2A 5X3

Not valid for current subscribers to Love Inspired Suspense books.

**Are you a subscriber to Love Inspired Suspense
and want to receive the larger-print edition?
Call 1-800-873-8635 or visit www.ReaderService.com.**

* Terms and prices subject to change without notice. Prices do not include applicable taxes. Sales tax applicable in N.Y. Canadian residents will be charged applicable taxes. Offer not valid in Quebec. This offer is limited to one order per household. All orders subject to credit approval. Credit or debit balances in a customer's account(s) may be offset by any other outstanding balance owed by or to the customer. Please allow 4 to 6 weeks for delivery. Offer available while quantities last.

**Your Privacy**—The Reader Service is committed to protecting your privacy. Our Privacy Policy is available online at www.ReaderService.com or upon request from the Reader Service.

We make a portion of our mailing list available to reputable third parties that offer products we believe may interest you. If you prefer that we not exchange your name with third parties, or if you wish to clarify or modify your communication preferences, please visit us at www.ReaderService.com/consumerschoice or write to us at Reader Service Preference Service, P.O. Box 9062, Buffalo, NY 14269. Include your complete name and address.

LISUS11B